Christmas in Holly

Gail Gaymer Martin

In his heart a man plans his course,
but the Lord determines his steps.
Proverbs 16:9 NIV

Chapter 1

" 'I am the resurrection and the life,' says the Lord, 'he who believes in me, though he die, yet shall he live, and whoever lives and believes in me shall never die.'"

Amanda Cahill closed her eyes and squeezed them together as hard as she could to control the stream of tears begging to be released. Her effort failed. They escaped in rivulets, rolling down her cheeks and leaving cool streaks against the warm autumn sun. She'd thought she'd cried herself dry since the day she'd received the call, but tears, like raindrops, often arrived without warning to dampen a sunny day. Today the sun hid behind her grief.

Her grandma's tenderness filled her mind, her gentle words always full of forgiveness. "Mandy, God forgives those who forgive. Let it go." *Mandy.* Only in Holly did she hear her childhood name. In Chicago, she answered to Amanda, but the nickname rang with familiarity in this place and gave her a sense of belonging.

She dug into her pocket and pulled out a tissue, then brushed away the tears. The pastor's words hovered in the background as she looked with tear-blurred vision at the bouquet of summer flowers adorning her grandmother's coffin—mums, snapdragons, foxglove, and a sprig of holly, her grandma's favorite shrub in her garden. What could be more fitting?

Other than two of her grandma's cousins, the mourners standing beside the grave were friends— neighbors, church family and business people on whom her grandmother had made a lasting impression. While her grandma's lonely days had ended, Amanda sensed hers had just begun. Her grandma was the only family she'd had left beside her mother, but that was another story. One she didn't want to think about today.

Shaking off her thoughts, she looked into the sky and watched the sun drift behind a cloud, shrouding everything in shadows. Yet a spark of light remained. Beneath the artificial grass and coco matting covering what would soon be her grandmother's grave, Amanda's father rested in peace beside her without the loss and sadness the world offered. He'd been a wonderful father. Amanda only wished her mother had appreciated him.

Beyond the mourners, monuments dotted the landscape of burnished leaves scattered on autumn grass. Beneath the trees, families had planted flowers now fading and placed mementos in memory of those they loved. So much love surrounded her. She longed to feel it.

The sun burst from behind the cloud, and Amanda lifted her face, drinking in the warmth. Her grandmother loved life, and Amanda knew she should celebrate and not grieve. She waited as the pallbearers guided her grandmother's coffin to the edge of the grave, and as the mourners filed past, some took a flower from the casket bouquet in remembrance.

The pastor's voice remained in her thoughts, a prayer for those left behind. Then the words she dreaded most met her ears, followed by the symbolic ping of earth the pastor sprinkled on the polished cherrywood coffin. "We commit her body to the ground: ashes to ashes, dust to dust; in sure and certain hope of the Resurrection to eternal life, through our Lord Jesus Christ. Amen."

Her grandma's two cousins lingered a moment before following the others to their cars that would take them to the house where a lunch would be served.

Watching them go, Amanda inched toward the casket, and as she bowed her head to say her last goodbye, a hand touched her shoulder. She turned, and her heart skipped. "Ty." Relief whispered through her, but seeing his face and the concern in his eyes opened the floodgates. She threw her arms around his neck and wept as his comforting arms held her close.

"I'm so sorry, Mandy."

Fighting the knot in her throat, she could only nod in response to his whisper. The scent of his aftershave flooded her senses, the same fragrance he'd worn since she could remember. Today she needed a friend and here he was. *Mandy*. The feeling rose again taking her back to her life in Holly before her world caved in. Before her daddy died. And when he did, Tyler Evans had been her rock then, too.

Ty held her closer, cradling her in a lullaby rhythm that soothed her aching heart. When her emotional outburst seemed under control, she eased back and looked into his eyes—sky blue eyes filled with tenderness— and slid her hand over his hair, the sheen of black patent leather. Her loneliness fluttered away.

He clasped her arm and guided her forward. Amanda stood beside the coffin, feeling his presence behind her. She rested her hand on the polished wood and breathed in the fragrance of the flowers.

When Ty eased back, she slipped a snapdragon from the bouquet and clutched it in her hand, then fondled the sprig of holly. "I love you, Grandma." Her voice had been a whisper. With one last look over the scene, tears pooled her eyes. She longed to have one more day to tell her grandmother how important she'd been to her. But wishes weren't part of real life. She sensed her grandmother knew. She touched the cherrywood again and stepped away.

Ty moved beside her, slipping his arm around her shoulders, and walked her across the grass.

She paused and gazed at his concerned expression. His full lips pressed together as if holding back his own emotion. "Ty, it's so good to see you. I wondered why—"

"I was out of town." He lifted his finger and brushed away her stray tears. "Out of town on business, and I just got in this morning."

Even hearing his voice put her at ease. "I knew you had a reason."

He drew her hand into his. "Had I known I would have excused myself to be here." He glanced toward the casket. "No one let me know."

Her chest tightened. "Things happened so fast, Ty, I didn't have time to think. I should have called you."

"I got here as fast as I could." He squeezed her hand as he slipped it away. "Your grandma and dad.

They always welcomed me like family."

"You were even better than family." She couldn't take her eyes from him, his tender touch, the curve of his mouth, the crinkles around his eyes when he smiled.

His gaze captured hers. "Your mother didn't come?"

A shudder rattled through her as she shook her head.

"I'm sorry, Mandy."

Drawing up her shoulders, she looked toward the last cars pulling away. "The church ladies are putting on a luncheon at grandma's house. You'll come, won't you?"

"You know I will."

"I'm glad. It's been so long." Amanda winced. Why hadn't she kept in touch when her mother had forced her to move away? Looking at him now made the question more painful. He'd been her support. A young man with aged wisdom. Ty always said and did the right thing. Pulling her gaze from his, she eyed her watch and motioned toward the black car behind the hearse. "The driver's waiting to take me to grandma's."

Ty's hand touched the small of her back. "Tell him I'll drive you home."

"You will?" She gazed at him again, drinking in the sight of him. "Thank you." She tiptoed and kissed his cheek. "You're the dearest friend in the world."

His eyes searched hers until a small grin broke through his serious expression. "You mean even your best friends in Chicago."

She shook her head. She'd never found anyone there as close as Ty had been to her. Today reminded her of how much he meant.

Ty tilted his head toward the driver. "You should let him know he can leave."

She agreed and stepped away, then paused to look at him over her shoulder. "Where are you parked?"

He motioned behind him. "The van. Bright red. You can't miss it."

Bright red. He'd driven the van from the hardware store. His father's business van had been his teenage wheels. A grin broke on her face, releasing the tension that had built up the past stress-filled days. She ran ahead to let the funeral attendant know Ty would take her home.

He clasped her hand and thanked her. "If you'd like any of the floral arrangements, you can drop by tomorrow. Otherwise we give them to nursing homes."

Remembering the many lovely flowers, her gaze drifted to three floral arrangements resting beside the grave where the workmen now stood, preparing to lower the casket into the ground. She turned away, willing her emotions to calm. So many lovely bouquets had been sent, some with baskets and one, she'd noticed, with an angel sculpture worked into the floral design. "I'll stop by in the morning."

"That'll be fine. We'll hold them until you can get there any time tomorrow."

Amanda thanked him, then turned her back to the sounds of the workman and headed for Ty's red van.

He stood beside the passenger door, one hand in his pocket, the other resting against the door handle. His tender expression calmed her, but beneath his expression, she saw something deeper, as if seeing her had rekindled the warm and sweet relationship they'd enjoyed for so many years. The same feeling had filled her earlier.

As he stepped back to open the door, she slipped her arms around his waist, resting her head on his chest. "I've only seen you once, maybe twice, since I moved away from Holly, and it's all rushing back."

He cupped her head in his palm. "I know."

His voice had a plaintive tone, and she assumed his thoughts were on her grandmother's burial. Her own melancholy rose again while she stiffened at the sound of the backhoe moving the earth into the grave.

Ty jerked his head, seeming to rouse himself from his own memories. "Let's go. They're waiting for you at the house."

As always, he understood her need to escape. She slipped inside the van, and Ty closed the door. After he'd settled onto the driver's seat and turned the key in the ignition, a golden oldie tune rose from the radio, a welcome distraction. The familiar song lifted her spirit. "Listen." She motioned to the radio and waited a moment. "Do you Remember?"

The haunting words of *Kiss From a Rose* floated from the speaker as Seal's velvety voice took her back to high school.

Ty glanced at her, then shifted into drive and pulled away.

Didn't he remember? A sliver of disappointment inched through her.

He turned down the volume on the radio, his eyes on the road. "We were sitting on the hill where the holly grows, and a stream of sunlight broke through the clouds as if God held a huge flashlight aiming straight at you."

Her disappointment scattered. He remembered. The

day reeled like a movie in her mind. "And I became poetic and said the light should be on you because you were like a lighthouse and made my dark times bright." The memory prickled up her arms.

"I remember." He gave his finger a shake at her. "Don't tell me the rest. I can't believe I was that sappy."

She could hear him singing the words of *Kissed By a Rose* to her that day. He'd touched her more than he knew. "It wasn't sappy. I thought it was beautiful. The best thing a friend could do when I was so depressed."

He reached over and rested his hand on hers. "I don't sing anymore so don't expect it."

"We'll see about that." Her heavy heart lightened, and for a moment, she reveled in the happier mood their conversation had brought.

She turned up the volume again, catching the last few lines of the Seal's nostalgic melody before it segued to the Backstreet Boys. Pictures flooded her mind—football games in the freezing cold, skating on Simonson's Lake, picnicking at Stiff's Mill Pond, and most of all sitting somewhere—anywhere— just talking. No girlfriend offered her the same sense of confidence as Ty had from the first day she noticed him in seventh grade. She trusted and appreciated his honesty.

"Look at all the cars. This is quite a tribute."

Ty's voice snapped her back from the reverie. Cars lined Park Avenue beyond her grandma's house and a few sat single file in the double driveway. The turnout touched her. "The church ladies are known for their generous funeral luncheons. I'm so grateful. I don't know what I would have done without so many people's help?"

Ty nosed his van into the driveway and turned off the motor. He slipped his fingers through hers. "It's a good town, Mandy. You remember." He gave her hand a squeeze. "Ready?"

She nodded, remembering more than she wanted. The town held fond memories. Her home life, not so much. "I'm ready."

He released her hand, slipped out of the driver's side, and opened her door before she could find the handle. She slipped to the ground and headed for the enclosed porch stretching across the front of the house. As she neared, she could see people seated inside. Ty opened the door, and she stepped in.

Most of her guests held plates filled with food, and the aroma floated through the doorway to greet her. Heads nodded and guests reminded her again of how many people loved her grandmother.

"Your grandma was a wonderful lady."

"We'll miss her in Bible class."

"Mr. Johnson and I are so sorry about your grandmother."

Some of the guests called her Amanda while others used her shortened name, Mandy. Some faces she remembered, while others she only recalled from the funeral home visitation or the cemetery. They shook her hand, gave her hugs, and wiped away their own tears. "Thank you for coming. Grandma would be very pleased."

Dena, one of the cousins, slipped to her side. "The ladies have a great spread in there. You should be very thankful."

She gave a nod, but her thoughts were on the

condolences from many, and a few probing looks from some. What would she do now? What would happen to the house? Where was her mother? She could only guess their thoughts.

As she neared the dining room, her grandma's next door neighbor stood in the archway, beckoning to her. "Mandy, come and eat."

Ty touched her arm. "Why don't you?"

"Come with me." She caught his arm. "You know these people better than I do."

"You know Edith Weston." He grinned as he tipped his head toward Edith. "She's flagging you to the table with a paper plate."

Amanda chuckled. "I can see that. Come with me." Again, she beckoned him to follow.

He nodded but didn't move.

Not wanting to ignore the neighbor, Amanda gave up and strode through the cozy sitting area to reach Edith's side. "Thanks for all you've done." She accepted the paper plate.

"We all loved Rose." Edith slipped her arm round Amanda's back. "I know you did too." She waved her to the table. "Now eat something."

Amanda eyed the array of food, her thoughts on Edith's comment. *I know you did, too..* Beneath it, she recognized a familiar insinuation. Her mother didn't love her mother-in-law, and the whole town knew it. The stigma bothered her even now. But she wasn't like her mother. Not one inch of her.

"Amanda."

Edith's voice drew her back as she approached with a stranger at her side. "Amanda, this is Lauren Rice. She lives next door on the other side." She motioned to the left.

Amanda extended her hand. "Nice to meet you, Lauren. Thanks for coming."

"I'm so sorry about your grandma. She was such a sweet neighbor."

"Thanks. I'm sure—" Before she could say more, a hand rested on her shoulder, and she knew who it was from his touch. "Ty, this is—"

"Hello, Ty."

Amanda's lungs constricted. She looked from Lauren to Ty. "You've obviously met."

Ty opened his mouth, but Lauren cut him off as she grasped his arm. "This man was so helpful when I moved in a few months ago. I needed so many little things done, and he stepped in and rescued me."

Amanda blinked at their familiarity. "Ty's good at rescuing women. He rescued me for years." The words flew from her mouth before softening the comment. She couldn't believe the sensation that plowed over and, even more, couldn't believe the snide comment that flew from her mouth.

She searched Lauren's expression, seeing nothing but a pleasant smile. "But then you know first hand." Amanda hoped she'd eased her earlier attitude.

Ty scowled. "The hardware carries the things that Lauren needed, and I helped her find a handyman."

Amanda wanted to sink through the floor. She had no hooks on Ty and never would have, other than friendship. Their relationship was precious. She'd never want to lose it. She managed a pleasant look. "That's what I meant. Ty is a very kind person."

She could see the woman's eyes flashing between her and Ty, and Amanda was grateful that Edith had

11

walked away without hearing her ridiculous comment.

"You need to eat, Mandy." Ty's voice had cut through the heavy silence.

She lowered her gaze seeing she still clutched the plate that Edith had given her. "You're right." She managed a grin as she walked away and ambled around the table, adding spoonfuls of salads beside a slab of ham.

Ty followed behind her, his choices piled higher than hers. When they'd each selected their favorite food, Amanda searched for a place to sit. Her feet hurt in the black pumps she'd grabbed from her luggage. They were new, and she should have known better.

"Let's check the back porch." She beckoned him to follow, and when Ty pushed open the screen, the chairs were empty.

"Good choice." He motioned her to sit.

She chose the swing and with a new abandon, she slipped off her shoes and curled up on the worn slats, once red, now mainly gray wood. Her head spun, and she tilted her head back, letting the silence remove the din from her mind.

Ty knew her well. He settled beside her, gave her knee a pat and remained quiet.

When she dug into her food, though delicious, swallowing became a challenge. Emotions knotted her throat. Too many people, too many decisions, and the worst, the unexpected reaction to Lauren's familiarity with Ty. She'd never been a jealous person, and with Ty, she had no right to be. She'd been away for many years.

"Not hungry?"

Amanda turned to Ty. "My stomach's hungry, but

eating is difficult with a lump in my throat."

"Don't force yourself. They'll leave leftovers. You can eat later."

She nodded.

He set his plate on the table beside his chair, then grasped hers and stacked it on his. When he settled back, he studied her a moment. "What was that about?"

"What?"

He didn't respond.

"I don't under—"

"Your comment to Lauren about my rescuing you for years. You sounded resentful."

The knot in her throat tightened. "I'm not resentful. Not at all."

"I've always helped you when you needed me, Mandy. I didn't know it bothered you."

He looked disheartened, and she searched for some way to explain. "I love that you've always been there for me. I'd never resented your help." She shifted nearer and reached for his hand, hoping to cover her utter shame for being so unthinking.

Ty studied her hand a moment before taking it in his. "You sounded different."

"I'm a mess today. Forgive me."

He rubbed his thumb over her fingers. "It's been a difficult week for you. I shouldn't have let what you said bother me." He released her hand and leaned back. "So, what are your plans?"

"Plans?" She shrugged. "I don't know."

"Are you staying in town for a while?"

She lowered her head, then raised it to look into his eyes. "Grandma left a will, and I'm the executor."

He gave a nod. "That makes sense. When do you

take care of that?"

"There you are." The two cousins trotted onto the porch, oblivious to Amanda's reaction. They continued to smile as if they hadn't interrupted. But Amanda realized she should have been more careful. Now wasn't the time to talk about the will, and she wondered if the sisters had overheard.

Dena's eyes shifted from her to Ty and back again. "You have company inside, Amanda, and many are ready to leave."

"Perhaps this isn't the time to..." Gwen faltered following a glare from her sister.

Though she flinched at the comment, Gwen's expression struck her harder. Amanda couldn't decide whether Gwen thought she'd found Ty and her in a romantic tryst or if she'd overheard her comment on the will.

Lowering her feet, she straightened her back. "I need to say goodbye to the guests."

Ty stood while she leaned forward and slipped on her shoes. Her feet gave a cry. Ty offered his hand to help her. The swing veered backward, then swung forward as she rose.

The sisters hung back, allowing her to enter the house first. Amanda sensed Ty had stayed behind. She didn't blame him.

When she looked around the large dining room, most of the food had disappeared from the table, and she heard the church ladies in the kitchen cleaning up. Uneasy that she hadn't been more sociable or helpful, she picked up a few dishes left on a lamp table near the living room fireplace and dropped off the dishes.

She ambled from place to place, saying goodbye to

the guests, and the more she listened to their reveries, the sorrier she became that she hadn't spent more time with her grandmother over the past years. Chicago wasn't a short jaunt. At least a five-hour drive stretched between Holly and Chicago. Over three-hundred miles. Flying took nearly as long with the airport waits and car rental.

Wrestling with her guilt, Amanda stood at the door watching the last of the guests leave except for the cousins and the ladies still working in the kitchen. She gathered a few more dishes and carried them to the sink where Edith greeted her with a smile. Perspiration beaded the neighbor's hairline and upper lip.

More guilt. "You're all working so hard. I can't thank you enough."

Edith waved away her words. "We're happy to help. Don't say another word." She headed for the refrigerator and tugged open the door. "I hope you're staying a few days." She gestured to the contents inside.

Amanda's jaw dropped. The shelves were filled with plastic containers holding leftover food. A month wouldn't be enough to clear out the contents.

"Some of it wasn't put on the table. The donations kept coming in, so we thought you'd enjoy not having to cook for a while." She shut the door, her eyes on Amanda. "You are staying a few days?"

She nodded, her mind reeling with too many things to consider and so many things to do. "For a while anyway."

"I'm sorry your mother didn't come."

Amanda swallowed her frustration and could only nod.

Edith opened her arms, and Amanda stepped into

her embrace. The woman smelled of lemon soap and disinfectant. She had attacked the kitchen with the energy of Mr. Clean.

"Now, if you need anything at all, don't be afraid to ask. I'm right next door." Edith gave her a "with-no-uncertain-terms" look.

"I will, Edith. You can count on it."

She patted Amanda's arm. "Good, and I'm sure Lauren will give you a hand, too, when she can."

Lauren? A queasy feeling rippled in her stomach. She'd acted so rude to the woman and needed to make amends.

As they were speaking, the other ladies said their farewells, then Edith, too, slipped off her apron and grabbed her handbag. "Remember, I'm right next door."

Amanda's heart squeezed with her kindness. "I'll count on you."

Edith beamed a smile. "Good." She turned and walked into the foyer where the cousins' goodbyes echoed into the kitchen.

Amanda peered at the room, cleaner than it had been when she arrived three days earlier. She puffed out a lengthy breath, searching for stamina to deal with the cousins who were apparently waiting for something. When she felt ready to face them, she raised her shoulders and stepped into the foyer.

Gwen ambled toward her as if she'd been a sentry waiting at the door for her appearance. "We're finally alone."

No. You're still here. Amanda squelched the feeling and forced a pleasant look. "I'm very tired. I'm sure you are too." *And I'm hoping you want to go home.* She wished her thought would sail into their minds.

Dena pressed her hands together. "Now we have time to talk."

Amanda's wish had failed. "Talk?" A squint tugged at her brows. "About what?"

Dena's eyes widened. "About the house and the—"

The conversation was not what Amanda wanted to face today. "I have no clue what'll happen to anything. There is a will."

The sisters peered at each other. Then Dena turned back, her eyes sparking. "Have you read it?"

"No, but I'll see the lawyer on Friday."

"And?" This time Gwen joined in.

Amanda's back stiffened. "And what?"

Dena's glare could cut metal. "We should have been invited to the reading."

Gwen eyed her sister's face and softened her expression. "Perhaps Amanda will invite us."

"It's not my responsibility, Gwen. Usually if the will has something in it pertaining to you, the attorney would have notified you. I assume you're not mentioned in the will."

Dena glowered while she scanned the room, her gaze darting from one piece of furniture to another. As if she'd found her answer, she crossed the carpet and rested he hand on her grandmother's secretary desk, touching the pigeonholes and a vase that sat on the mirrored ledge.

Dena lifted the lovely delftware. "Well, now, I think—"

Amanda bit her lip, feeling the wash of emotion sweeping her away. "Dena, we just buried grandma today. I don't want to start tearing up her house this afternoon."

"No one mentioned tearing up the house."

"You know what I mean, Dena." Amanda drew in a lengthy breath. She had too much on her plate today, and it wasn't food.

"Let's talk later. I'll check with the attorney. If you want to read the will, I'll see if I can pick up a copy for you."

A distrustful look swept over both of them, but Amanda had no other answer. She hadn't read the will either.

Dena sucked in a breath. "Fine, then. We'll talk tomorrow, but in my opinion, we're kin and should be at the reading."

Gwen remained silent. She lifted her handbag from a nearby chair, gave Amanda another probing look before scurrying onto the porch. Dena followed. Relief came when she heard the thwack of the screen hitting the door frame. They were gone.

Amanda stood a moment to get her bearings. Alone at last. Alone? Ty? She hadn't seen him since she'd come inside. Concern grew as she looked into the unoccupied living room, then rushed through the dining room and kitchen. Empty. She swung open the door to the back porch and saw him sitting on the swing. He looked up as she stepped onto the plank floor.

"I'm so sorry." Her heart thudded against her breastbone. "I was afraid you'd gone."

"I'd thought about it, but I would have said goodbye." He glanced at his watch.

Amanda moved to his side and hugged him. "I'm glad you didn't. I would have been disappointed." She sank beside him, slipping off her shoes and stretching her legs. "I feel as if I've been in a car wreck." Like cars at rush hour in Chicago, her mind came to a halt, and she dropped her face in her hands.

Ty drew closer, his voice a whisper. "It's everything toppling over you at once, Mandy. You're strong, but you can't carry it alone."

She gathered her wits and raised her head, thanking God her stalwart friend sat beside her, encouraging her to reconnect with her commonsense. "You're right. The whole thing crashed over me for a second."

He brushed his finger beneath her chin as a frown wrinkled his forehead. "What happened in there?" He tipped his head toward the house.

She shook her head, hating to review it all. "The funeral, the guests, the kindness, the confusion, the questions. It's too—"

"Shush." He slipped his arm around her shoulders. "It's too much for one day."

She nodded. Words weren't necessary with Ty.

He used his heel to rock the swing, and they sat in silence, time ticking past, in a soothing rhythm. She rested her head on his shoulder, as his familiar fragrance served as a balm to her aching heart and mind.

Ty lowered his head against hers, and her stomach chose that moment to rumble a noisy protest. He jerked upward with a chuckle. "I think something's telling you you're hungry."

"It's not very subtle, is it?"

He pulled his arm from her shoulders, stood, and reached for her hand. "You need a meal. You didn't eat a thing earlier."

Ty led her back inside, plopped her onto a kitchen

chair and held up his hand to stop her from speaking. "Sit and I'll fill your plate."

She watched him locate a plate from the cabinet, and after two tries located the silverware drawer. She grinned, seeing him look so domestic. His strong arms flexed as he opened cabinets, and his broad shoulders gave her pause. She'd so connected with Ty from the past, she'd failed to appreciate the man he'd become. Her pulse gave a kick, and it surprised her.

She followed him with her eyes, and when Ty opened the refrigerator, his jaw dropped. "Whoa. You have food enough here for a month."

"I could start a soup kitchen." She'd seen so many in Chicago but guessed Holly didn't have one. The small town nestled among rolling hills, farmer's fields and woodlands seemed an unlikely setting for a soup kitchen.

During her rambling thoughts, Amanda watched Ty fill her plate. He remembered her likes and dislikes, and it made her smile. He placed the heaping plate in front of her, then poured her a glass of iced tea and set it beside her plate.

"You don't like sugar, right?"

She didn't.

Ty settled at the table, his hands folded in front of him as he watched her eat. After a few minutes, he rose, sliced two pieces of cake, and joined her for dessert.

Her stomach groaned at the amount of food she'd consumed so quickly. She rested her fork on the plate and pushed it aside. "Delicious."

"Good, I'm glad you ate." He grinned, wiping cake crumbs from his lips, but the grin was short-lived. "How long will you be staying? We were interrupted the last time I asked."

She pictured the two sisters charging onto the porch, and now after their concern about the will, she understood their eagerness to stick around. "I see the attorney in the morning, and then I'll know what I have to do."

His anxious look shifted to curiosity. "You don't know what's in the will?"

She shook her head. "Grandma never talked about her will, and I figured if she wanted me to know, she'd tell me. She'd asked me to be executor a long time ago. That's it."

He rested his palm on the back of her hand and gave it a pat. "She trusted you."

"She did, and I trusted her. I didn't have much to rely on in my family after Dad died." Tears burned in her eyes again, and she brushed them away.

Ty gave her a long look. No words. He understood.

"The day I arrived, I spent all my time with the pastor and the funeral director. It wasn't until yesterday morning before the visitation I called the lawyer." She placed her free hand over his, enjoying the closeness. "I'll know the details soon." Amanda sensed she was talking to herself.

"Would your grandma leave anything to your mother?"

His question felt like a weight on her shoulders. "I doubt it, but I don't know."

A moment of silence passed before Ty's head bobbed up, slipping his hand from hers. "My folks are leaving a gift of money to the church in their will. Maybe your grandmother would leave something to the church. Or what about those cousins?"

The comment struck her funny bone. "Gwen and Dena? They'd be thrilled. They cornered me after everyone left?"

His eyebrows lifted. "You're kidding."

"Nope. That's why it took me so long to get back to you. They probed me with questions, but I didn't have anything to tell them." Her mind shot back to what he'd just said, and she weighed Ty's suggestions as possibilities. "I doubt if Grandma left the cousins anything. She called them her curious cousins. I think it was a nice way to say they always had their noses in someone else's business."

Ty chuckled.

But the other option struck her. "You know, maybe grandma did leave it to the church. She had no one else but my mother and me. She hasn't seen my mother since she moved away, and I live in Chicago."

A far away look settled in his eyes, but she didn't ask. Instead, the cousins' faces loomed in her mind. The vision made her smile, and the more she pictured them learning the church was heir to the estate the funnier it became.

"Maybe grandma did just that, and it would serve the cousins right."

She expected him to laugh, but he didn't. Instead the look on his face concerned her. What had she said?

Chapter 2

Ty lifted his head and saw Mandy studying him. Her words rang in his ears. *I live in Chicago.* A fact he knew, but for the past hours since he'd seen her, he had removed that barrier from their friendship. Hearing her say it had struck him harder than he would have thought possible.

"Is something wrong?" Her smooth brow furrowed. "You seem upset."

"Not really." He looked away again, unable to admit what really bothered him. "I've been thinking about my Dad. He's been having some health problems." Another real concern.

She drew her hand from his and pressed it against her chest. "Is it seri—"

"It's not serious. At least I hope not. Some heart flutters." As he tossed off her question, reality reminded him that death knocked on everyone's door eventually. Ty and reality sometimes walked different roads. He'd lived so long in what-ifs.

"But that's nothing to ignore."

Mandy's voice jarred Ty from his thoughts, and when he focused, her concerned expression had deepened. He wanted to apologize for his distraction, but he hoped she hadn't noticed. "Dad had a doctor appointment this morning. Mom went with him, and that's why they didn't make the funeral. You know they would have been there otherwise."

Mandy waved away his words. "No apology necessary. In fact, I feel badly I missed seeing them at the visitation."

He leaned back, surprised at her statement. "You mean they didn't...? Mom said they—"

"No. No." She shook her head. "They came, but I'd gone to grab a bite to eat. I was disappointed when I came up and I saw their names in the visitor book. I wish they'd stayed. Seeing them would have given me a lift."

An idea charged through Ty. They both needed a pleasant distraction. "We could take a ride to their house."

Her eyebrows lifted. "Today?"

He shrugged, trying to read the sound of her voice with one word. "Well, you haven't seen their..." He'd never been edgy with Mandy, even when his feelings had grown, and he knew hers hadn't. He'd lived with it to maintain their friendship. That had meant everything to him. And he'd clung to hope. "You haven't seen their new house, and—" Shadows had grown beneath her eyes, and the sparkle had vanished. "Mandy, what am I thinking? It's been a long day and—"

"No, Ty. It's a good idea. I'd love to see them."

His spirit lifted. "You're sure? Don't do this to make me happy. "

She gave a decisive nod. "If I sit here alone, I'll be depressed."

That struck a chord. The joy he'd experienced seeing her had knotted into a ball of confusion. He drew up his shoulders. Life had gone on when Mandy left twelve years earlier. It would go on no matter what happened.

"I'll give them a call." Ty pulled out his cell phone, hit speed dial, and when his mother answered, he proposed the visit. Her animated voice gave him the answer.

"She's thrilled." He shot Mandy a grin, pleased that his idea had eased the tension he'd begun to experience. He listened to his mother's proposition on the other end of the line, then covered the mouthpiece. "She's invited us to dinner tonight."

She nodded without giving it thought.

Ty tried to get control of his emotional roller coaster. "We'll see you later, Mom."

He could hear the pleasure in his mother's voice as she began to list the menu. He hated to cut her short, but he couldn't concentrate. When he finally disconnected, he slipped the phone into his pocket. "Thanks. You've made her very happy."

"She's a good mother, Ty. I hope you appreciate her."

Mandy's own roller coaster etched on her face, a father wounded by his wife's distance and a mother who lived in a private world that let no one in. His own mom opened her arms to everyone. He'd been blessed.

"Ty?"

His head snapped upward as he pulled his mind in focus.

"You're daydreaming." She grinned.

He lifted his shoulders. "Sorry. Mom gave me the menu, and I was thinking you could feed them with your stuffed refrigerator." Though his mind had been elsewhere, the thought had flashed through him when he was on the phone.

Mandy pushed back the chair and stood. "You're right. Maybe, I should invite them—"

"No. Don't even think it." Ty rose and slipped the chair beneath the table. "You don't want any more company today. You need to get away from here for a while." Her expression let him know she was relieved.

"Do I have time to change?" Mandy gestured to the dark suit she'd worn to her grandmother's funeral.

Tangled in his own crazy thoughts, the sorrow of the funeral had nearly left his mind. "Take all the time you need."

She left the kitchen, and he heard her footsteps climbing the stairs. Ty rinsed off the dishes and set them in the sink, then ambled into the living room and settled on a love seat in front of the broad fireplace. He gazed around the room, admiring the workmanship of the sturdy old house. Who would own this house now? Who would live inside these walls? The same dream floated in his mind. Mandy. He could picture her planting flowers in the beds, pruning the holly bushes that her grandmother loved, redecorating the rooms, and making this house her home.

He rested his head against the cushion, willing his body to relax. He'd allowed his emotions to get carried away with his worn-out thoughts. Two good friends, but one who'd had stronger feelings. He'd feared that acting on them would kill their relationship, a friendship that had become precious.

He jerked his shoulders upward and rose, striding to the enclosed porch. Windows had been opened allowing the guests to enjoy the breeze. He guessed the house didn't have air-conditioning. So many of the older homes didn't. If Mandy lived here, she would—

Stop.

Ty leaned on the windowsill and peered at the maple tree that shaded the house. Years ago they'd climbed that tree, he and Mandy. He'd goaded her into it. She'd always feared heights, and he'd tested their friendship, promising her that he would stay behind her and catch her if she fell. Stupid kids. She could have broken her neck. Without a thought of danger, they'd mounted the thick branch, him behind her, and they'd sat among the leaves and talked about their hopes and dreams.

He'd never opened up to anyone like he did with her. His buddies wanted to pick up girls and sneak booze. That's what they talked about. Ty? He'd poured out the beer when they weren't looking and tried to hide his personal decision to save himself for marriage. That's what his parents and God expected. Mandy believed the same. They'd vowed they would both remain chaste until they fell in love with someone and married. Their values bonded them even more deeply.

The memory knotted in his chest as he turned his back on the tree. It had grown taller the past twelve years, and today they would need a long ladder to get anywhere near that branch. Those innocent days struck him, and today he would need more than a ladder to undo what he'd done since Mandy left. When Mandy moved away, time and age had changed him. The relationship faded with distance, and so did the vow. But now that he saw her again, he wished he could bring back those days and the bond they'd had.

"Ready."

He turned hearing Mandy's voice behind him. He caught his breath. She had changed into white pants and a pink top with a rounded neckline and lacy-looking trim. She looked pure and innocent. Pure. It smacked his conscience. Gathering his wits, he rose. "You look like an angel."

She shook her head. "You have me mixed up with my grandma. She's the angel now."

He approached her and slipped his arm around her shoulders, then gave her a squeeze. The closeness washed over him as he guided her to the door, and though he wanted to guard his heart, Ty sensed he had a fight on his hands.

♥

Lauren Rice wiped off the kitchen counter before picking up her glass of iced tea and taking a sip. Since arriving home from the funeral luncheon, her mind had tried to deal with Amanda's sudden sarcasm.

When she'd come home from next door, a frown had settled on Lauren's face, and now she lifted her brows trying to relieve the stress. She had a headache, and the tension knotted in her neck. She carried her glass and headed into the living room. Peering through the picture window, she noticed all the cars had gone from the Cahill house except Ty's red van. Ty? The problem with Amanda occurred when she'd spoken with Ty. She shook her head, trying to rid herself of her thoughts.

Though Edith Weston seemed to be fond of Amanda, Lauren hadn't deciphered her yet. Amanda had seemed pleasant enough when they'd met, but that had changed. What made the difference?

Ty's good at rescuing. Amanda's snide tone of voice ended her hope for a new friend. She rubbed her temple to ease the thrumming.

Lauren shifted to step away from the window but halted when she caught a glimpse of Ty and Amanda coming through the front door and heading for the van. They appeared to be talking—not holding hands, no arm around her—so what was the problem? She'd suspected she'd somehow threatened a romantic interlude. Yet she saw nothing like that in their behavior now.

She carried her tea back into the kitchen and slid the glass onto a shelf in the refrigerator. Talking to Edith might help her understand, but she needed a reason to knock on her door. "Hi, Edith. What's up with Ty and Amanda?" That wouldn't work. Edith had no idea that she'd been tangled in the hopeful dreams of a relationship with Ty. The guy was great. Everything a woman could ask for.

Since she'd gotten to know him, Lauren wondered why he'd remained single. Later she suspected he might be a widower, and she'd posed a few question—subtle ones—but Ty didn't say much. The longer she knew him something about him told her he'd never married. A good man like Ty had to work to remain that way. And now Amanda's reaction?

An idea glimmered in Lauren's thoughts. She dug through her pantry and found a plastic container Edith had sent over with cookies from a new recipe. It was a throw away, but Lauren couldn't see tossing something still useable in the trash. Remembering her mother had taught her returning an empty container was rude, she stood a moment gazing around the kitchen. Nothing struck her. Desperate, she opened the refrigerator and spotted her answer—a quart of big fresh strawberries. Edith's container held the berries perfectly. Lauren snapped on the lid and headed for her neighbor's.

When Edith answered the bell, surprise shown on her face. "Lauren, come in." She pushed open the screen and welcomed her inside. "What's in your hand, there?" She stepped back and eyed the covered bowl.

"Strawberries." The declaration shriveled Lauren's confidence. Strawberries sounded stupid, especially since they weren't home grown.

Edith's grin stretched as she reached to accept the berries. She eyed the plastic bowl as if recognizing it. "You remembered."

"Remembered?" Lauren went blank, unless she was referring to the container itself.

"The angel food cake."

Relief. "Yes." She chuckled, recalling that Edith had mentioned baking a box cake in case it was needed for the funeral luncheon.

"What's better with it than strawberries and topping?" Edith turned away and headed down the hall. But at the kitchen door, she paused to look over her shoulder. "Would you like a piece?"

"No. Thanks. I'm still full from the luncheon." She followed Edith to the kitchen door, her purpose pressing on her mind like a weight.

"It was a lovely luncheon. A fine tribute to Rose." Edith lifted her focus from the inside of the refrigerator.

"I'm sorry Mandy was so stressed. She's the sweetest young woman usually."

Lauren's brow knitted, and she tried to hide her frown.

Edith eyed her over the refrigerator door. "She seemed a little abrupt, didn't you think?"

Though fearing Edith suspected the purpose of her visit, Lauren was grateful she didn't need to initiate the conversation. "I did wonder. I thought maybe I'd done something wrong or said something. She was fine until Ty joined us."

Her comment raised Edith's eyebrows. "Don't know about that. Ty and Amanda are the dearest of friends. Have been since junior high school."

"Friends." She tried to keep her voice level though her pulse had kicked up a notch.

"That's right. What's that called? Planton...?"

"Platonic?"

Edith snapped her fingers. "That's it. I never saw a thing like it."

Tension faded, and Lauren released a whew.

Edith's eyebrows lifted again, curiosity in her eyes.

"Whew!" She said it again to cover her mistake. "It's wonderful to have such a great friend, and I'm relieved to know I didn't do anything to upset Amanda."

Edith shook her head. "Don't you worry about that. I'm sure Amanda doesn't even realize what happened. She's stressed from the funeral, I'm certain."

"I'm sure that's it." Lauren managed a grin, not quite as certain as she let on. The more she thought about her silly excuse to talk with Edith, the more she wanted to make her escape. With her question answered, she searched for a genial way to say goodbye.

♥

Amanda gazed from one smiling face to the other, her heart still warm from the greeting she received. Ty's father looked great, despite his heart problems, and Amanda guessed that Ty would still be a good-looking man when he reached his sixties, too. Seeing his parents took her back to the good times she'd had in their home, although this was a new house. She'd toured it when she arrived and chuckled that the house was bigger than the one where Ty had grownup. So much for downsizing.

The table held a Thanksgiving bounty, and today was a plain October weekday. Amanda smiled at Ty's mother. "Thanks so much for inviting me. It was so thoughtful."

Ty's mother gave her a tender smile. "We wouldn't have it any other way." She motioned for Amanda to sit and she joined her. "This feels like times when you and Ty came in from swimming in the pond or sitting under the tree studying." She shook her head, tears rimming her eyes. "Look at me getting sentimental." She waved away her emotions. "Let's enjoy the food while it's warm."

When Mrs. Evans stretched her arms from her sides, Amanda grasped her hand and Ty's in the other before bowing her head for a blessing.

Dishes were passed—pot roast with meat so tender it had shred into pieces, rich brown gravy, mashed potatoes, and vegetables that included Michigan tomatoes—nothing like them in Chicago. Amanda had thought she'd eaten enough at the funeral luncheon, but this meal filled her heart even more than her stomach.

Silence hung around them, disturbed only by the click of their forks against the plate and the rattle of ice cubes in their water glasses. The first voice to break the quiet was Ty's father. He rested his arm on the table edge, his fork still in his hand. "What happens now, Mandy?"

The question split through Amanda's comfortable feelings. She struggled to control her frown.

"Roger." Mrs. Evan's hushed but firm voice followed his like a bullet.

"I'm only asking, Dot." Ty's father lifted his arched brows. "We all feel sad Rose is gone, but adults face reality, and Trina isn't here to help her daughter. Maybe we can help."

Amanda flinched with the reference to her mother.

Mrs. Evans flashed her an apologetic look.

She let the question settle in. "I see the attorney tomorrow." Amanda had hoped to avoid the sadness she'd coped with all day here in the Evan's home, but Ty's father's concern fit his nature. He'd always cared about her needs. She filled them in on the little she knew and even mentioned the cousins.

"You'll be staying in Holly for a while then?" His mother's hopeful voice edged into the conversation.

"That depends on what the attorney says. I know what grandma's cousins are wishing." She managed a halfhearted grin.

Ty slipped his hand over hers and gave it a squeeze. "Let's enjoy Mandy while she's in town. She'll make the right decision."

"Here. Here." His father clapped his hands.

"What kind of work do you do in Chicago, Mandy?" Dot's gentle voice followed her husband's louder one.

"Graphic design." Amanda's shoulders relaxed with the change in topic. "I freelance for magazines and advertising firms. I create layouts for ads or brochures. Design logos. All kinds of things."

"That's impressive," Mr. Evan's smile grew. "Do you have one of those corner offices with a great view? I see those places on TV shows."

Amanda grinned back. "Most of my work can be done at home."

"Then if you stay here, you can still work. That's good news."

Ty's voice surprised her. He'd been quiet at dinner.

"At times, I attend conference meetings learning about the target audience and to brainstorm project ideas, but I can work in my PJs at home most of the time."

Everyone chuckled, but Amanda noticed something out of sync in Ty's eyes.

Dot rose and began gathering dishes, but Amanda shot from her chair. "Please, let me do that. You cooked a wonderful meal. Let Ty and me clean up."

"Good idea." Ty stood and steered his mother toward the living room. "We'll have things taken care of in a jiffy."

Dot resisted, but as her husband joined her, he took over and guided her through the archway while she gave them an are-you-sure look over her shoulder.

Amanda sent her an encouraging nod as she and Ty stacked dishes. When they reached the kitchen, she studied Ty's broad back as he piled the load of dishes on the counter. Once again, he caught her off-guard. He was more handsome now than good-looking, and he'd gained a maturity that added to his attractiveness, but he was still Ty. The familiarity squeezed her heart, and yet at dinner, she recognized a look of longing in his eyes. Again it reminded her that time had passed.

Maybe alone in the kitchen, she could find out what that look was about.

Chapter 3

Ty heard Mandy's footsteps behind him, and he moved aside, giving her room to set down the dishes. His skin prickled, smelling the familiar fragrance that always followed her. Shampoo? Lotion? Perfume? The aroma set him in an orchard of wildflowers surrounded by fruit trees. He drew in the scent and closed his eyes, picturing the amazing days of their youth. "I hope my folks aren't driving you crazy."

"Crazy. Not at all." She turned on the tap water and swished a soiled dish with a brush, then paused, the water still swirling down the drain. "They remind me of some of the good times back then."

Back then? His chest tightened. "It's been amazing having you home."

"I keep reminding myself it's not the same, is it? Things change. We're different now."

"Are we?" He studied her face, hoping she'd back down on her comment. He'd stayed pretty much the same, always wishing he'd find another girl like her. Someone he could talk with and be open with. Be himself. With others, he felt as if he should try to impress them.

"Come on, Ty." Her eyes searched his, her head shaking as if she were unbelieving. "You haven't sat here in Holly and let life pass you by. You're enjoying life, aren't you? Having fun."

He stared at his shoes, wishing he could answer from his heart.

"How about a girlfriend?" She paused a minute and grinned. "Or do you need me here to play matchmaker?"

His head jerked back. "Matchmaker? I don't need any help with—"

She held up her hand. "I'm talking about high school. You never wanted to date anyone. I had to force you to ask someone out. The girls fell all over you, but you didn't see them." She poked her finger into his chest. "You didn't even go to the prom, remember?"

Remember? He'd never forget. He'd finally found courage to tell her how he felt, but she had accepted a date with another guy before he'd had a chance to ask her. Thinking back now, he could kick himself, waiting too long, so afraid she'd laugh and say no. He was her confidant and friend, not her boyfriend.

"I even tried to fix you up for the prom, but you didn't follow through." Her smooth forehead crinkled with her playful scolding.

Ty grasped his emotions by the neck and twisted his mouth into a grin. "Proms weren't my thing. Can you picture me in a tuxedo?"

She drew back, her gaze traveling the length of his body. "Yes, I can. You would have been so handsome. Any girl would give an arm to go to the prom with you."

"What about you?" The words shot from his mouth, causing the food he'd just eaten to churn in his belly.

"I had a date, silly." She swatted his arm, but a new look spread over her face.

Ty tried to read the expression but failed.

Mandy turned away to rinse the dishes. "Forget the prom. Let's talk about now. You must have lady friends." She piled the plate on the others and gazed into his eyes. "You must date and..." She paused as she glanced at his ring finger. "Haven't you found someone special? Ever thought about marriage?"

"Have you?" He managed to steal his emotions and give her a matter of fact look. "I'm only thirty. Still wet behind the ears, as my mom used to say."

She grinned and tilted her head around to eye the side of his head. "They look pretty dry to me."

Ty managed to laugh and hoped it sounded sincere. "Don't I look happy?"

"I suppose." Her gaze probed his. "But I still don't understand why?"

"Why what?" He knew but he had to think of an answer.

"You know what I mean. You've lived in town all these years with single women at your beck and call."

"You mean Lauren?"

She winced. "I wasn't thinking of anyone in particular."

He wished he hadn't brought that up.

"I mean you have opportunities. Chicago isn't the greatest place to meet a man when you don't hang out in bars or use the Internet."

The Internet. He couldn't picture her searching the

Internet to make a connection. All she had to do is smile and any man would fall on his face.

"So what about you?" Mandy's gaze caught his without a blink. "Why are you still unattached?"

Her voice cut him, as his lungs deflated. "Never found a girl like you, Mandy." He managed a playful grin.

"Right." She rolled her eyes before she chuckled.

He wanted to tell her he'd loved her then, and a piece of him still did, but he couldn't utter a word.

♥

Amanda left the attorney's office, her head whirring. The possibility had never crossed her mind, but with her dad and her grandma's sister already deceased, it all made sense. What would she do now with her grandmother's property?

As she strode to her car, she checked her watch. It was later than she expected, and she'd promised to be at the funeral home to pick up flowers before noon. She unlocked her sedan and slipped inside. Ty probably wondered why she hadn't called. He'd offered to go with her for the flowers.

Ty. Their last conversation still burned in her ears. She'd pushed him into a corner on the dating issue and being single. Why? She'd asked herself over and over without an answer except one she didn't like. Not at all.

More guilt. Ty had dedicated his time to her. They'd been closer than best girlfriends ever were. He knew her family's situation. He'd empathized with her sadness. Understood her hurt. He'd made her laugh and been her favorite companion.

What had she done for him? Moved away. Dragged

away by her mother and the new husband was more like it. Her father had barely settled in the ground. Amanda had turned her back on Holly and everything in it. But Ty? He'd been different...and she'd let her bitterness destroy what was precious to her in the town. Ty and her grandmother.

She'd taken a number of years to come to grips with her anger at her mother and to return to Holly to visit her grandma. Ty had been away at college and a job somewhere. They'd met one time in town and jumped into a bear hug as if life hadn't torn them apart.

But life moved on. She'd begun work in Chicago...and she'd let go of Holly and everything in it. Her chest tightened with the harsh memory. She'd let Ty go.

Amanda pulled out her cell phone and hit Ty's number. His voicemail clicked in. She bit her lip, wishing he'd answered. "Ty, I'm leaving the attorney's office now. I'll stop home to change clothes, but if you don't get this soon, I'll go alone for the flowers. I know you're working." She clicked off, slipped her phone in her bag, and shifted into reverse.

The attorney's message rang in her ears. Her grandmother had left her everything. Her mind spun again with decisions she'd have to make, and she could hear the cousins complaints since the attorney hadn't invited them.

A brown envelope containing the will peeked from the top of her purse. Rather than argue, her cousins could read the words themselves. She'd listened with her jaw hanging to her chin, and it still sagged with her shock. She had her grandmother's bank account to settle, the house to sell, her grandma's belongings to dispose of, and somewhere in there, she had to work since she'd just taken on a new project with a producer, designing DVD jacket covers.

Her eyes grew heavy with the weight of tasks spilled out before her. She almost wished she'd told the funeral assistant to forget the flowers. She'd rather go to the house and take a nap. Nap? But that wasn't her. She never napped, but she certainly felt like one now.

The colorful bouquets and the angel sculpture filled her mind. She'd pictured the sculpture in her grandmother's garden, and the floral sprays would look beautiful in her grandmother's house. A lovely vase and a pretty basket that she'd admired settled in her thoughts. Edith deserved a bouquet, and Amanda had wanted a couple arrangements for the church. Her stomach rumbled, and though she'd considered stopping to eat after seeing the attorney, at the moment, she had no interest in food, although her tummy hadn't noticed.

When she pulled down Park Avenue, her heart dropped. A car had parked in her grandmother's driveway, and she recognized it as Dena's. As she pulled in front, both doors opened, and the cousins stepped out, their arms folded waiting for her like hawks seeking their prey. She dug deep for patience and fortitude before opening the door and slipping from the sedan.

"Dena. Gwen. Good timing." She strode forward, planting as pleasant a look as she could muster.

Gwen drew up her shoulders. "We've been waiting over an hour."

Amanda figured as much. "I'm glad you caught me then. I have another appointment so I'll be leaving soon."

Dena hadn't moved. Her arms bound tighter against her chest as if she'd planted herself on the grass as a sentry. "We're here to see the will."

Amanda dug into her bag and pulled out the folded document. "I have a few minutes. Would you like to step inside?" She kept the will in her hand and turned her back on them, but the sound of their footsteps against the concrete alerted her that they'd followed.

Arguing or blaming or whatever they'd concocted in their minds knotted in the pit of her stomach. Amanda could debate with the best of them during her project sessions. Her confidence had grown as she'd established herself as a qualified graphic designer, but wrestling over her grandma's belongings and money tore her to pieces. Ty tripped through her thoughts. If he arrived soon, his presence would help monitor their conversation. More than that, he would bolster her confidence. He always had.

She held open the door, allowing the cousins to march in ahead of her. Breathing in the fresh air, she took her final step into the house. Fresh air. Ty's face hung in her mind. Ty had always been her fresh air. Yes, he'd given her confidence, and with him, she breathed hope. What was it that she loved about him? Her heart tugged as she pictured him beside her, his arm around her shoulders, his twinkling eyes teasing her. He'd been faithful.

Amanda pulled away from her thoughts, faithful lingering in her mind, and closed the door. Before she could set down her bag, Dena's hand appeared in front of her. She glanced down at the will, then released it to her.

Dena stood in one spot, plowing through the legalese of the document while Gwen hovered beside her, tilting her head from one side to the other and adjusting her glasses. Trifocals, Amanda guessed. Gwen would just have to wait. Dena had an eagle's grip on the document.

Glancing at her watch, Amanda found her manners. Though she needed to head to the funeral home soon, being gracious to her grandma's cousins came first, as hard as it was. "Please have a seat. Can I get you something to drink?"

With a cautious look, both of the women asked for iced tea and settled into a chair in the living room while she made her escape to the kitchen. She leaned against the counter and lowered her head as a prayer filled her mind, asking God to help her face all that was ahead. When she opened her eyes, she stood a moment, realizing how little she leaned on the Lord. Religion had never been much of an issue in her home growing up, but her grandmother's strong faith had served as an example and solace.

Releasing a lengthy breath, Amanda filled two glasses with ice cubes and tea, then grasped the sugar bowl and two spoons before she carried them into the living room. When she came through the door, the sisters' heads were bent, their voices low, and Amanda waited for their blast of comments.

Two pair of eyes raised, no words spoken as she handed them the glasses and offered them sugar. They needed something to sweeten their disposition. She backed away and sank into an easy chair, her mind a whir.

Dena lowered the document in her lap. "I can't

believe your grandmother would have done this without some devious hanky panky."

Amanda's head jerked upward. "Devious hanky panky? Dena what are you insinuating? I don't like the sound of it. I had no idea Grandma had left me everything. I'd thought she might leave it to the church, but—"

"But what about us?" Gwen's softer voice sliced Amanda's sentence.

"I don't know, Gwen. I can only guess that Grandma wanted it to go to her closest kin, and that's me." Amanda gasped for air. "I'm as surprised as you are."

"Really." Gwen's voice carried a hint of doubt.

Amanda fell against the chair back, too weary to attempt to convince her.

"Now hold on. Let's not play games."

Amanda ducked Dena's caustic tone. She'd had enough. She rose, located her handbag, and dug inside until she found the card. "Here." She strode toward Dena her hand outstretched. "Take this. It's the attorney's business card." She swallowed the bile rising to her throat. "If you want to argue with him, please do. I can't change what the will says. Grandma signed it, and I wasn't the witness. I'm only the executor."

Dena snatched the card from Amanda's fingers. "I'll do just that."

Gwen sniffled and wiped her eyes. "Dena, don't cause trouble over—"

"Trouble?" Dena's voice pierced the room. "I'm trying to make sense out of this will. You and I know that Rose would have left us something."

"But—"

Dena's glare ended Gwen's comment.

Amanda sank back into the chair. "Look. I need to get my head together. I had no idea what this would entail, and now I have so many things to do. But please know I'm not going to keep all of Grandma's belongings." Her eyes raked the room, trying to recall what Dena had admired the day of the funeral. "You'll be welcome to take some mementos once I—"

"Mementos?"

Dena's sarcasm scratched Amanda's patience, but she continued to ply her thoughts until she remembered. She rose and grasped the delft vase. "Dena, take this with you, and Gwen, if you see something in the room you'd like, please take it. After I've had time to get my mind in order, you'll be welcome to more of grandma's things, but not today." Tears pushed behind her eyes, but her determination halted them. She refused to break down in front of the women. "I'll call you in a few days. I promise."

With a dark look, Dena clutched the vase while Gwen wandered around the room, lifting items and putting them back in place. Finally she came forward, clutching a glass paperweight. "I'd like to have this." Gwen held out the lovely orb displaying a bouquet of flowers. Amanda clutched it, watching the blossoms enlarge and fade depending on how it was held.

"It's beautiful, Gwen." Amanda placed the paperweight into her hands. "You're very welcome to it."

Dena took a step toward the door before she paused. "What's Rose's money situation."

The blunt question prickled down Amanda's back. "I don't have the figures. I'll take care of the bank and

45

other business next week. The funeral expenses need to be paid first."

Gwen had already passed Dena and stood next to the door, her hand on the knob. "Thank you, Amanda."

Dena bustled across the room to join her. "We'll be in touch next week."

I'm sure you will. Amanda bit her tongue. "I'll know more then."

Gwen opened the door, and Amanda grabbed it and held it as the women crossed the porch and started down the outside steps. When she looked toward their car, her heart leaped. Ty's red van was pulling into the driveway. She noticed the cousins giving it a look, then chattered to themselves as they scurried to their car. When they reached it, Dena eyed her from over the roof.

A puff of air shot from Amanda's lungs. She hated to think the worst, but she suspected Grandma's cousins would try to gain revenge somehow. She didn't even want to think about it.

♥

Ty spotted the women bustling from the house, and he could only guess that the visit had been strained. The will. And from their look, they weren't the recipient of whatever they thought might be theirs.

Had he noticed the car earlier, he might have waited down the street. The one without glasses, Dena, he thought that was her name, gave him a stare that could blast a duck out of water, and when Mandy's face came into view, it validated what he'd already guessed. He sat a moment, sending up a prayer that God's will be done, but an earlier prayer contradicted it. Ty wanted his wish to come true. He longed to have Mandy back in his life even for a while. Maybe for once, he could do things right.

Pulling the handle, he pushed open the door and slid from the van. Sometimes he forgot he owned a good-looking car, but the van seemed wiser if they were picking up the flowers. He strode up the porch steps while Mandy waited by the front door. He hated bringing up the subject of the cousins, but he could see it was on her mind. "Bad situation?"

She tried to grin, but the strain was too evident. "I sent them home with a token gift."

She meant something by gift, but he wasn't sure what she meant. "What kind of gift? Like a check?"

"No, but that would have made them happy. I gave one a delft vase and the other a paperweight. I'll give them a few things, but I need to make decisions and go to the bank. I have to take care of all that next week."

Next week. At least she'd stay for a while, and hopefully he could... No. He had to stop. So far nothing led him to believe that Mandy even suspected how he felt about her. He closed his mind to his thoughts. "The church or you?"

"Me. No one else." She looked into his eyes and all he saw was confusion. "Not one thing for my mother. I thought maybe something, but—"

"You were dubious."

She shrugged. "I know, but Grandma was so forgiving she might have left something small. I had no idea what she had in mind. She didn't talk about dying or wills. But she did talk about heaven and seeing Grandpa again."

"Forgiveness is one thing." Ty's thoughts slipped

back to the hurt Mandy's mother had caused the family and the gossip. "Rewarding her for the mess she caused your grandmother doesn't seem probable."

"I know."

She lowered her head and Ty did what seemed natural. He wrapped his arms around her back and drew her close. She rested her head on his chest and drew in a lengthy breath.

"I have so much to do. So much to think about, and I don't know where to begin."

Ty swayed with her in his arms, wishing he could take away her worry. He wanted to do something, but he had no idea what he could do? "The attorney should have given you some direction."

"He handed me a list of things I needed to handle, and the funeral director gave me the death certificates I ordered. I guess that's what I need at the bank."

"Take a deep breath, and step back. You've had too much fall on you all at once. It's almost the end of the week, and what you can't do now, you can do next week. I'll help you anyway I can."

She gave him a squeeze and reached up to kiss his cheek. "I know you will."

The touch of her warm lips against his skin amazed him. He longed to turn his mouth to hers, but he knew this wasn't the time or place. He had much work ahead of him and only a short time to move in that direction.

Settling beside him, Amanda gazed into his eyes. "You've always been wonderful, Ty. I said it yesterday. You're the best friend I've ever had."

Though it was a compliment, Ty wanted so much more. He nuzzled his chin against her hair. "What do we do now."

"I said I'd pick up the flowers this morning." She drew back and glanced at her watch. "It's almost two." She lowered her arms from him and tugged up her shoulders. "I'm thirsty. I need something to drink, and then we can go to the funeral home, okay?"

"Fine with me." Anything was fine with him when it came to Mandy. He followed her into the kitchen and leaned against the counter, his gaze sweeping the room, facing all this was hers.

She opened the refrigerator door and pulled out a pitcher of tea. "Want some?"

"No, thanks." He studied her again, longing to ask the question that had clung in his mind since he'd seen her yesterday. "Have you made any decisions?"

She turned to him, the empty glass in her hand. "Decisions? About the house?"

"The house and—"

"I'll need an appraiser, and I need to know what condition the house is in."

Ty's spirit lifted as his hope rose. "Like maybe infested with termites?"

She swatted at him and sloshed the tea. "Don't make me laugh." She swiped the counter with a dish cloth and put the pitcher back in the refrigerator. "Like a bad roof, electrical problems, plumbing disasters waiting to happen. I want to know the house is in good condition."

Ty's pulse jogged, and a smile tugged at his mouth as his hopes rose. "Are you thinking of moving back to Holly? Living in the house?"

Her back straightened, and surprise lit her face. "Live here? No. My life's in Chicago, Ty. I'll be here a week or two, I suppose, but I couldn't come back to a small town. I'll sell the house."

I couldn't come back to a small town. Ty's smile shattered as he reined in his emotions, He pictured her yesterday, so happy to see him, and she would never know how amazing she'd made him feel when she opened her arms to greet him. They stood so close he could almost feel her heartbeat, but now an ache filled his chest. She had no idea how deeply she'd stabbed him with her abrupt statement. She'd become a big city girl and he remained a small town boy. He had to stop his thoughts, so he grappled for something to turn the conversation around. "You can't rush into any decisions, Mandy. Give it time."

"I won't change my mind. My work is in Chicago. Sure, I'm a freelancer and can do graphic design anywhere as long as I have my computer and the Internet, but my contacts are there, and...my life is there. I have an apartment and friends."

The knife twisted deeper. Earlier she'd said she had found no one in Chicago as good a friend as he was. He studied her face, wondering if he knew her as well as he'd thought.

"You look surprised."

Her voice cut into his thoughts. "I shouldn't be, I suppose."

Concern etched her face. She looked helpless and lost, and despite his disappointment, he drew her hand into his, wanting to release the tension.

He had a week. Maybe two. He prayed the time he had with her would make a difference.

Chapter 4

Amanda hoped that she'd seen the last of her two irritating cousins, but before she had a chance to organize her thoughts, they appeared again, wanting to know what her grandmother had left them. She stumbled over her words, trying to explain that she had many things to take care of before she knew what things were worth and what she would do with it all. "I promise, Dena, you and Gwen that I'll make sure you take some of Grandma's furniture or jewelry if she had any, or…" She lowered her head and caught her breath. "You see, I don't even know what Grandma had that has value or what I might be able to share with others."

Dena reared her head, her nostrils like an angry horse. "What do you mean you might be able to share? We're relatives too, and—"

"We're cousins, Dena." Gwen grasped her arm. "Amanda is her granddaughter. We have no legal right to anything from her grandmother."

Dena reared back again. "What do you mean no right? We have—"

"No right." Gwen leaned into her face. "Why can't

you understand that? What did you do for her dad's mother? We're related to Amanda's mother's side of the family."

"But we knew her." Dena's pitch reached the ceiling.

Amanda's eyes widened. "Dena, please. A lot of people knew my grandmother. Her neighbors were dear friends who did a great deal for her, and I certainly want to thank them with a remembrance." She had to clamp her mouth shut, longing to ask what they ever did for her grandmother, but she didn't want to sink to that level and she let it drop.

Gwen beckoned to Dena. "Amanda has too much to do to sit and chit chat, so—"

"Chit Chat?" Dena's volume flew sky high.

Her patience limited, Amanda flexed her palm. "Let's not get into an argument. Gwen is right. I have too many things to do before I know what I can do with Grandma's house, furniture, and everything else she—"

"Like her money?" Dena's voice chopped through her sentence.

The room fell silent. So silent, Dena's fluttered breathing echoed in the room. Gwen frowned at her, but Dena ignored her and rose, muttering as she grasped her handbag. The only words Amanda heard as Dena stomped out were two words—stealing and lawyer.

Gwen shook her head, a flush growing on her face. "I'm sorry, Amanda. Really sorry."

"So am I, Gwen, but I'm not blaming anyone. An inheritance can cause loving people to turn into money-grubbers. I forgive her. And I am sorry that Grandma left everything to me. You know that I'm going to have to deal with my mother who was ignored also. I understand why, but my mother never will face the truth."

"I don't envy you, Amanda. I wouldn't want your job right now. Take it slow, and I know you can handle it all."

Though she thanked Gwen for her confidence, her own evaluation wasn't that positive. If she could walk away, she would, but that wasn't a choice.

"Take a break, Amanda. Everything will fall into place." Gwen gave her a hug and moved to the front door. She gave her a goodbye wave, as Amanda plopped into a chair and closed her eyes.

Once she calmed, she rose and wandered to a cabinet against the wall. The shelves held some of the knickknacks she'd referred to with the cousins, but it also had a line of drawers and a set of doors. She pulled open the top drawer and found a pile of table clothes and a box of doilies. She closed the drawer and pulled open the door. Inside she spotted a few photo albums, she guessed. She pulled the top one out and her heart skipped, seeing photos of her as a child, often with her grandmother. A number of people she didn't recognize, and then when she turned the next page, an unusual photo of her mother dressed in more formal clothing as if going to something special. She looked for writing on the back of the photo but there was nothing.

Her curiosity rose and she grasped the other album and returned to the chair she'd been sitting in earlier. She flipped page after page, studying each photo. Some were strangers. Others were a few people she knew, her grandmother and granddad, her mother and some she guessed were neighbors. One photo stopped her cold. Her mother stood smiling into the eyes of a man who had his arm around her, and it wasn't her father. She knew a little about her mother and father's relationship but not enough to make sense. She longed to know why they had married. She guessed one of the elderly neighbors might know something. One day soon she had to ask.

♥

Ty sat in the hardware's office working on a list of products he needed to order, but instead of finishing the list, he thought of nothing but Mandy and what she needed to either live in or sell her grandmother's house. As the idea of her living in the house settled in his mind, his pulse skipped, sending ripples of hope flooding his brain—that is, if he had one.

Whenever Mandy's image filled his thought, he stepped away from reality and clung to his dream, a dream he'd had forever. Yet the dream often dug out questions. Can a dream come true? Can best friends ever open their hearts to love. He'd tried to drown the longings he had always felt for Mandy. If he'd had the courage to let her know his feelings years ago, their relationship might have been different, but after all the years they were good friends—best friends—he had no idea how to make the change to true love.

If he acted on it now, he could lose her, since he knew so little about romance. He didn't know which way to turn. Asking one of his male friends would never work. They would laugh if they realized how naïve he was.

He tossed the pencil on his desk, bumping his leg against an open drawer as he bound up and turned his back to the list. All he could think of was Mandy. He stood a moment to garner some commonsense, but that seemed impossible. With his head lowered and his shoulders rounded, he headed into the store and paced through the aisles, trying to organize his thoughts.

In the paint aisle, Ty stopped at the color samples while a new idea struck him. Mandy would need help getting the house ready for sale or to live in. He stared at the shades of white and other colors that might add interest to the look of the house. The shutters could be painted a shade of brown or green, perhaps. What would Mandy like best?

"Hi, Ty."

His pulse skipped when he heard the feminine voice, but when he turned, Lauren stood near him, eyeing the paint samples too. "Lauren, what are you planning to do with paint?"

She grinned. "I was wondering the same about you."

He managed to cover his guilty feeling as if looking at paint for Mandy was cheating on Lauren. He had never looked at Lauren with any thoughts of romance. Even the word made him grimace. "I'm working on my order list. These paint samples go fast."

"I suppose they do, especially when someone has a whole house to paint." Her gaze probed his, and he caught the innuendo.

"True." His voice caught in his throat. "Can I help you find something, Lauren?"

"Not really, I found a couple of things I came in for, and when I saw you, I realized you'd been in hiding for a while."

"In hiding? Not really. I've had lots on my min— lots of things to get in the store for the holidays.

November's in eight days. Thanksgiving will be here soon, and then Christmas."

"Yes, they both will and sooner than we expect." A crooked grin stole to her face. "I believe last year I invited you to our Thanksgiving dinner."

He nodded, digging deep to find something thoughtful to say. "How could I forget?"

"That means you enjoyed yourself, I hope." Her smile broadened, and she studied his face as if looking for something in particular.

Ty managed to control a grimace while he struggled to grin, a pitiful grin, he suspected. "It was nice of you to invite me." Yet now he needed to be blunt and fast. "This year I'm—"

"Ty, please don't eat alone, you are welcome to—"

"Thanks, Lauren, but this year I have plans."

"Oh." Her face drained of color and her smile flipped upside down to a frown. "I thought you..." She studied his expression and faltered. "I guess I thought wrong."

He nodded, hoping to let the conversation die. "But thanks anyway, Lauren."

She stood facing him as silent as a statue. "Have a nice day, Ty." Without a smile or wave, she turned toward the doorway and left.

Ty's chest weighted with the hurt he saw on Lauren's face. Men looked at situations differently from women, and it took him a while to realize she had feelings for him. But no matter what he did, those feelings never dented his heart. The only woman who made an impression was Mandy, and he sensed it would be that way forever.

Redirecting his mind, his plan before Lauren's

appearance had been to drop by Mandy's house and bring some of the paint samples which he was still clutching. Though he had no idea what she might need to paint, he scanned the various choices and pulled out a few shades of beige and blue. She loved blue, and he wondered if it was because his eyes were a shade of blue. She often mentioned it. He slipped the paint samples in his shirt pocket and let his clerk store manager know he was leaving.

Outside the late autumn sun warmed his back, reminding him how Mandy's presence had always warmed his spirit. Her hair, the color of autumn's hues, took away his breath, shades of sand, honey and gold. She meant more to him than he could explain or even understand.

When he reached his car, he slipped into the driver's seat and sat a moment, rehearsing some dialogue and hoping he sounded casual.

But once on the road, he calmed. Mandy would never be surprised that he showed up to help her. That had been his life, a life he loved, and one filled with purpose.

When he neared the house, reality struck him like a stone. Lauren lived next door to Mandy's grandmother's house. It hadn't bothered him years earlier, but while Mandy was living in Chicago, Lauren made sure she had her foothold whereever he was. He sensed she wanted to be a friend as Mandy was, but it didn't feel the same. Often, she came off like a stalker. He didn't want to see her that way, but an eerie feeling crept through him on occasion.

Mandy had parked near the garage, but before pulling in, he glanced toward Lauren's windows. He didn't see her, so he relaxed and turned into the driveway. He disliked sneaking into the house, but Lauren made him feel guilty for no reason. Maybe, he was. But guilty of what?

Chapter 5

Mandy's frustration rose to a pitch. She'd spent the day making a list of rooms in the house that needed work. Though she thought it would help her, instead the work multiplied and seemed impossible. She couldn't stay in Holly forever, and she didn't have money to throw away.

A noise caught her attention, and she faltered before going toward the large front window to look outside. A smile touched her lips when she saw Ty heading for the door.

She'd already reached the knob when he knocked, and she flung open the door. "Ty, what are you doing here?"

"Are you really asking me that?"

Her jaw dropped before she gathered herself. "You have to work at the store."

He stood on the porch without responding, while she pulled herself together. "Come in, Ty, and I realize that was a dumb question." She stepped back and beckoned him inside.

"Not dumb exactly. More like stupid." He grinned

and slipped his arm around her shoulders. "I had to come. I have always showed up when I think you might need some help or at least support. I know this is a big job for you."

"That's too true, Ty. I don't know which way to turn. I made a list of things I should do. That took me most of the day, and then when I read everything I'd scribbled on the paper, I panicked."

"You panic? I can't believe that."

"You'd better. You know I don't lie."

He tightened his arm around her shoulders and drew her closer. "Tell me what's on the list and let's see what I can do to help you." He softened the hug and guided her toward the sofa. "You can't do everything in a day or even a week, Mandy. And can you hire some of the work out to professionals?"

She sank onto the sofa cushion wanting to give up. "I hate digging into my savings, and though Grandma left some in her will, I think professionals would take most of that. I need to do as much as I can myself. Although, I do have another choice."

Ty's expression darkened. "You do have a choice. Live here yourself and take your time refurbishing the house?

"No. I have to go back to Chicago." She glowered at him. "The other option is to sell it as is. I thought that—"

"Mandy, no. You don't want to do that. The house would sell well if you did a few things to refurbish it. Don't throw away its value by selling it as is."

"Ty, I gave this thought. If I use Grandma's money or mine to modernize the rooms, I fear I'd lose more than what I could gain. The house is a bungalow. It's rather small."

"Yes, it's smaller than a ranch house. But not everyone wants a ranch. They're larger and that means more upkeep. Ranches."

Mandy shook her head. "That's too much for me."

"See, I told you." Ty sat beside her and patted her arm. "You need a bungalow just like this one."

Her head swiveled, her eyes searching his. "Ty, I need an apartment which is what I have in Chicago. That's what I need."

He clamped his lips and didn't respond for a moment. "Sorry, Mandy. I shouldn't tell you what you need. You're strong enough to stand alone and know what you need." His chest ached when the words flew from his mouth.

"No, Ty, I'm the one that's sorry. I've always expected you to advise me and help me make difficult decisions. I shouldn't have jumped on you like that." She shifted closer and rested her head on his chest.

He lowered his gaze, and tilted her head upward, fighting his desire to kiss her, but when he focused, tears dampened her eyes. "You've been under lots of stress, Mandy. Between your grandmother's death and your mother not showing up again, plus those cousins and now me, I—"

"Ty, don't put yourself in that list. You've been one of the best friends in my life. I am stressed. And Thanksgiving's nearly here and I haven't made any plans. I just thought of it earlier today. I suppose I'm not very thankful this year."

He raised his hand to her cheek and brushed his fingers over her soft skin. "Hush, you need a break. My folks are going to visit relatives out of town, so let's plan something for Thanksgiving. How's that?" As the idea left him, for some reason Lauren fluttered through his thoughts. He had lied to her saying he had plans." He released a ragged breath. He had plans now.

"Thanksgiving is still a few weeks away, but if you want plans, I can try to cook something, Ty, but I have no idea if I can handle a turkey or—"

"My idea of planning something made no reference to you, Mandy, or about cooking a turkey dinner. I had something totally different in mind. How about having Thanksgiving at the Holly Hotel."

"Holly Hotel?" Her face brightened. "I've had lunch there, and once I went for afternoon tea. That was interesting, but never a dinner, especially Thanksgiving dinner."

"Then let's experience something new. I'll call now and make sure we can get a reservation. I'm sure they book up fast." He pulled out his cell phone, and then grinned. "I suppose having the phone number would be helpful." He asked Google, and when the number appeared, he clicked on it and heard the ringing.

Mandy's grin remained, and when the hotel answered, he smiled back. "I would like to make reservations for Thanksgiving Day. Is that possible?" Relief swept over him when he heard the response. He looked at Mandy and winked. "Great. I'd like dinner for two at three." The positive response lightened his thoughts. "My last name is Evans and thank you. We look forward to Thanksgiving at the hotel." He looked at Mandy and gave her a thumbs-up. She nodded while a faint grin sneaked to her sweet lips.

He clicked off the call and reached out to draw Mandy to his side. "Problem solved. Dinner at three.

They have turkey with stuffing, pork shank and more."

"Dessert?" She poked him with her elbow.

Ty drew her closer and added another wink. "Would I take you anywhere without dessert?"

"Never." Unable to control himself, he bent over but questioned his action. Instead he kissed her forehead.

Though surprise lit her face, she didn't comment but gave his arm a pat.

Ty wasn't sure if she were disappointed or pleased. He hoped she accepted the innocent kiss. She didn't react so rather than say more about it, he changed the subject. "Thanksgiving distracted me from the real reason I came."

Her eyebrows lifted. "The real reason? What reason?"

Ty snatched the paint samples from his shirt pocket. "I'm bearing gifts." He grasped her hand and placed one paint sample at a time into her palm."

"Ty, what a lovely gift." Her words barely got out before she chuckled. "I've never received anything so amazing."

He stepped back, keeping his serious expression. "You see, I do know you well, and I always find the perfect gift." Reality caught him by surprise, and he faltered. "No more silliness, I came here to help you, and all I've done is waste part of your day with this foolishness."

She lifted her hand to his cheek, reminding him of his kiss. "I needed silliness, Ty. I'm overwhelmed with seriousness and I don't think I can handle much more."

"Then I'm glad you took a break. Let me know what colors of paint you need, and I'll make time to help you. And don't argue with me. I am going to help."

"Why would I be surprised to hear you say that?" She pressed her index finger on his lips and stretched up to plant a kiss on his cheek.

Startled by her reaction, a seeming approval of his kiss, he dragged in a breath and rose. "I'll get going now, but call me when you select colors and I'll be back to help." He didn't wait for her response. He pulled himself up, gave her a wave and headed for the door, reliving the touch of her soft lips on his cheek.

♥

Mandy finished the window trim in what had been her grandmother's bedroom and stood back admiring the white windowsills against the pastel blue walls lifted her spirit. She made progress, and as she worked, her thoughts distracted her from the many questions piling in her mind. Should she only paint what was absolutely necessary and let it go, or should she paint it as if she were going to live there. Her back straightened when that question struck her. Why think that? She would never live full time in Holly. It had been a place she visited since her home was in Chicago.

Once she pushed that question out of the way, her next one was why did Lauren keep popping into her thoughts, and even more important, why did she feel guilty. But that reaction, she knew. She'd learned Lauren had invited Ty to her house for Thanksgiving, and when he picked her up, she saw Lauren looking out the window. She wanted to flaunt her relationship with Tyler, but that wasn't fair.

Fair? A lot of things weren't fair. She could never

have more than a friendship with Ty, because she would soon return to her apartment and friends in Chicago.

With that thought of leaving Holly again, questions gave her a nudge. How much had she missed her friends and apartment since she'd been gone? Her memory reeled, searching for an example which never came. She hadn't missed anything. No matter what she did or tried to tell herself, she always missed Ty. The truth triggered a hollow feeling in her chest. No matter how hard she tried to live without him, she missed him when she was home in her big city world.

"How're you doing?"

Mandy jumped hearing Ty's voice. "Take a look." She used the paint brush as a pointer. "Do you like the color now that I have the trim done?"

"It's very nice, Mandy. I like it especially because I know you love the color."

"It's more than that, Ty." She longed to hand him a mirror, but none were handy. "You don't see your eyes as often as I do, and I look every time I see you. They're one of the things I lov—like about you."

The word-switch sent a ripple down his back. He gazed into her hazel-colored eyes as his chest tightened. "Thank you, Mandy, but I'll trade you for your color."

She drew back. "My color" He shook his head. "They're brown. Plain old brown."

"Brown with flecks of yellow and gold. Sometimes, a flash of green. You need to take a better look."

She released a playful moan and looked away. "Maybe one day, but not now. I'm too busy."

Ty's smile faded. "Right, you want to start another room so you can get this job done. I don't blame you.

Painting isn't fun."

His comment struck her, and she didn't understand. When the job was done, she'd go back to Chicago. She'd thought he wanted her to stay in Holly. Ty always made references to their fun times together, but his comment confused her.

He quieted and picked up a clean brush. "Which room's next? Living room? Kitchen?"

She stood a moment not sure what she wanted. "I've ordered new kitchen appliances. I suppose we should—"

"Good choice. Let's get the room ready for the delivery."

"It's the beige paint. The cans are sitting over there against the wall." She waved her hand toward the paint cans she'd purchased in his store.

He studied the cans and picked up two gallons of beige and headed into the next room, while his thoughts remained on Mandy's hazel eyes and how much she meant to him. He'd acted like a jerk, a royal clown who waited too long to tell her his feelings, and it irked him that he'd lacked the courage to admit the truth."

Mandy followed him and stood a moment before heading for walls below the counters. "I'll work on this since it's low, and I need these walls done before the appliances arrive. They should be here in about three days."

Ty gave a nod and grasped the ladder. "Or you can start the trim on the windows while I work on the upper part of the wall." She didn't argue so he opened another paint can, gave it a stir with the stick and set it beside her and then climbed the ladder to begin his job. As he worked, he glanced at Mandy, loving her closeness and yet kept apart by a ladder and paint cans.

He eased back and studied his paint job. Pleased that the paint was covering well, he dipped the brush into the paint again, but then stopped. His mind had wandered, and when he looked, he realized Mandy was standing on a wobbly step stool to reach the top of the trim. He stayed quiet, trying not to scare her, but he feared she was going to lose her balance since the stool she'd used shifted with her every move.

Without a word, he started down the ladder, and as he set the brush on the paint can, his heart skipped. "Mandy hang on." He darted toward her as her brush fell, and she followed with a shriek. In a flash, he grasped her as she toppled and held her in his arms until her feet reached the floor.

She clung to him, her body shaking against his chest.

"You're okay." He pressed her against him, hoping to provide a sense of security, but she didn't calm until he remained quiet and stroked calming circles on her back. When he felt her relax, he eased her down until she could stand on her own. "Okay, my love, I believe your career on a ladder or stool has ended."

"No, Ty. I can't get this done without it. I was careless."

"You were on a step stool that has seen better days So no more chances. You can paint everything you can reach from the floor." He shifted her focus to his. "Listen to me. No more climbing."

"Ty, I'm an adult, you can't tell me—"

"But I can. One bad fall and that's it. You could break your arm or be injured badly, and then be out of commission much longer than you say you can be here.

I'm doing this for your own good. I'm tall and I've worked with ladders all my life. So, I think you'd be wise to listen to me."

"But if I'm not back to Chicago soon, I can lose my job, Ty."

"No, you can't. You're a solid worker. You're here and getting your work done. They like you and know you do your job. If they didn't, you'd have been staying in the office and not given the opportunity to work from home or from Holly. You told me that."

She raised her shoulders and let them drop. "I guess that's the last time I'll tell you anything."

He grinned. "Why, because I'm right?"

Her weak frown faded into a grin. "I shouldn't trust you. You hold everything over my head."

"That's because I'm taller than you. I told you that."

She swung her arm and gave him a swat as her smile grew. "You frustrate me. Did you know that?"

"Then good. That's been my goal all of these years."

She shook her head but couldn't hide her smile. "Okay, you win. No more ladders or step stools.

He grasped her hand and drew her to him. "Let's sit a minute before we're too filled with paint to sit anywhere."

She shrugged, and with her hand in his, she followed him to the kitchen chairs. "Ty, how long is this going to take to get everything done?"

"I'll help you more than I have, and let's do the hardest rooms first. We'll finish the kitchen and then do the two bathrooms. When we're done with those, the hardest rooms are finished. We'll still have the two guest bedrooms, living room and dining room, but they look pretty good." He slipped his arm around her shoulders. "And by the way, you do too."

Her brow wrinkled. "I do too...what?"

He chucked her beneath her chin. "You look pretty good."

She lowered her chin with her head swaying. "I suppose that needs a thank you."

"Not really. You just look really good to me."

"Ty, you drive me crazy."

"Now, that's a short trip." He couldn't stop his chuckle. "But anyway, that's my goal."

She gave him another swat, but this time, she giggled. "How did it happen that I continued to be such a good friend of yours?"

"Lucky, I guess." And as he made the silly comment, his heart skittered with the truth.

♥

Though she managed a faint grin, Mandy let Ty's response fade away. She'd always been able to contain her emotions with him, but recently her control had slipped away, and her reaction to his comments and playfulness clung to her like plastic wrap.

"I need to get back to work, or I'll be here through Christmas." She walked to the paint bucket and picked up her brush.

Ty joined her, shifting to his paint can and brush. "You mean *we* need to get back to work, Mandy. This isn't a one-man job." He eyed the wall above the counter where he had been painting and climbed the ladder. "Would it be that bad to be here through Christmas?"

"Yes, it would." She froze hearing her words snap

at him like a snapping turtle.

"Sorry. It's none of my business." Ty turned away and dipped his brush into the paint.

Though she should have apologized, she remained silent while he finished the wall without a word.

She hated what had just happened. As in the past, she looked to Ty for support and encouragement. Sometimes he would ask if she needed some suggestions or help on making decisions. Today he remained silent.

While she tried to concentrate on painting, her eyes didn't cooperate. With quick glances, she could tell she had offended him, and her discomfort grew. An apology was appropriate, but the words stuck behind the lump in her throat while tears blurred her sight. She slowed and then stopped, fearing she would make a mess of the wall.

"Mandy, are you okay?"

"I'm fine."

He turned away with no response for a moment. "No, you're not. You have tears running down your cheeks." A weight pressed against his chest. "I wish I could take my question back since I fear I hurt you asking about Christmas, but it's too late, so all I can do is say I'm sorry."

"I'm fine, Ty."

He climbed off the ladder and set the brush on the paint can edge. "If you call that fine, I guess I need to accept it, but I don't believe you."

She wanted to rebel. Throw the paint brush at him. Scream. But she stifled the emotions riffling through her. She tried to focus on the paint, but she couldn't forget Ty's reaction, and she chilled, when she saw him put the top on the paint can and walk off with the brush. She'd upset him as much as he'd upset her, and yet she had no reason to be upset. His question made sense. She had no plans for Christmas though she assumed she'd find one of her coworkers without plans either, but...

"Mandy."

Ty's voice ended her thoughts. She turned and struggled to think of something meaningful to say, an apology or anything to ease the moment.

"I'm going to leave now. I'll try to get back, but I do have to order some Christmas items for the store. I usually have a variety of trees, ornaments, and other Christmas decorations, and if I don't order now, they won't be in stock when people start wanting them." He stepped back but then stopped. "Please don't work too long. I worry that you might have another near fall and this time no one is here to catch you."

"I'll be fine, Ty." The words sounded empty and over-used. She wasn't fine and hadn't been. "Thanks so much. You finished that whole section and that was a big job. I appreciate it more than I can say."

"No problem." He gave her a nod and headed toward the back door.

She understood. He worried about having paint on his shoes, but he didn't.

The room became silent when he was gone. The tears she'd fought earlier flowed down her cheeks and she climbed down the couple of the stool's steps to the floor. Filled with emptiness, she struggled to breathe. "Ty, what did I do? You're my true best friend, and I treated you like an unwelcomed stranger." How could she treat her dearest friend that way? The tears broke into sobs and she slipped off her shoes and hurried to the living room where she flung herself on the sofa and wept.

♥

Ty stared at the order form for the tenth time hoping he hadn't forgotten anything. With his head spinning and filled with Mandy's teary face, his frustration grew. "I give up." He threw down the pen and shot up from the desk chair, clutching the forms as he marched into the store to find Matt. He spotted him without trying. "Matt."

The store manager turned around, his expression giving him away. "Something wrong, Ty?"

"Nothing with you." He hurried to Matt's side and handed him the order forms. "Would you look over these and see if I missed anything important?"

Matt looked from him to the forms and back. "You want me to...? Are you okay, Ty? You look stressed."

Without going through the whole troubling story, Ty managed to find an answer that was the truth but not the whole truth. "I'd appreciate it, Matt. For some reason, I feel as if I'm forgetting something."

"I'm happy to go over it. No problem." Matt's focus remained on the forms. "I'll have it done soon."

Ty dragged his fingers through his hair. "That's good. As long as we can get the order out tomorrow, I think we'll be okay."

"That won't be a problem. And since I'm taking care of it, why don't you take a break. You've been in the office working on this for hours. In fact, did you eat lunch?"

Ty shrugged. Since his words with Mandy, he wasn't sure about much of anything. "Maybe you have a point, Matt. I think I'll take a break and—"

"And go out to lunch. Get some air." Matt rested his hand on Ty's shoulder. "I can handle the store. It's not like the Christmas crowds are here yet."

"True. I need to talk with a friend, too, and maybe this is a good time."

Matt gave him a revealing glance. "The woman you've been helping, I'll guess. You haven't mentioned her for a few days. Did she go back to—ah—oh, right, Chicago?"

Ty's stomach twitched. "Not that I know of. I suppose she's still getting the house ready to sell."

"Sell, huh? I know you two were good friends for years. I thought maybe she'd stick around for a while at least."

Ty shrugged again rather than admitting that's what he hoped too. "She can be hardheaded."

Matt shook his head. "Go ahead, Ty. I think you two need a healthy talk. Maybe you can sway her to—"

"I doubt it. One time in our lives, she asked for my opinion, but not anymore. As I said, she's bull-headed" Ty stepped back and eyed the check-out counter. "I'll get going and I'll be back before closing. Not sure when but—"

"Ty, I can close the store. You have things on your mind and that's more important. Go ahead. I'll be fine. I've closed the store many times."

"Thanks, Matt. I won't worry about it. If you need me for some reason, call. Okay?"

"I will. Now, get going." Matt gave him a playful pat on the shoulder.

Ty managed a grin and headed toward the door.

Chapter 6

Mandy caved onto a chair, her hands shaking and her thoughts cold and dark. Her mother's phone call rattled her, and she dreaded the upcoming encounter. Her head weighted with how to handle the situation, and once again, she needed to talk with someone who would understand, but the only person who knew her well and understood her relationship with her mother was Ty.

And Ty had walked out on her more than a week ago, and she deserved it.

Again, tears blurred her eyes. If she didn't feel boxed in by her grandma's house, now her house, she would have packed and returned to Chicago, but— Her head lowered with the weight of the truth. She couldn't do that, not leave Ty without asking forgiveness.

A thump sounded in the back of the house, and she jumped, concerned about what it was, but before she took a step, Ty's voice greeted her. "Mandy? Where are you?"

She faltered, confused as to what to say or do. "I'm in the living room, Ty." She didn't move as she tried to control her emotions and confusion.

Ty appeared and stopped when he saw her. "What happened?"

His question surprised her. "Why are you asking?"

"Mandy, I know you to well not to see that something has happened. Upset you, actually. Is it me?"

Tears broke free and rolled down her cheeks while she tried to get a grip on her emotions. "It's not you, Ty. You're the answer to my prayers."

He stepped closer but still held his distance. She couldn't stop herself from running to him and wrapping her arms around his chest. "I'm so sorry, Ty. I've been a jerk in all this confusion. You've helped me so much, and I did nothing to let you know how much I appreciate your help. You've always been my partner— my security, and I treated you—"

"That's over and done with, Mandy. What happened now? Today?"

"My mother called and is coming here."

"She knows about your grandmother's death, then?"

"She didn't mention it, but she must know. Someone told her, and my best bet is Dena. I doubt if Gwen would have let her know."

Ty ran his hand down her arm and wove his fingers around hers. "Let's sit and talk about this, but I do think Dena telling her makes sense. She wants to put pressure on you and I'm sure Dena knows your mother will do that."

"I know." She followed him to the sofa and sank into the cushion. "I'm about ready to give up on the house, Ty. I can do a quitclaim deed in the name of my mother and Dena. They can fight over it and do what they want. My hands will be free of the problem, but before I do, I want to look for anything that I would like to keep in memory of my grandmother."

"I understand why you're talking quitclaim deed, Mandy, but I'm not sure that's wise. Your mother and Dena did nothing for your grandmother, and if they had been important to her, they would have been in her will. And neither of them will be pleased with sharing the house. They'll cause you as much grief with that plan than ignoring them."

"You're right, and on top of that mess, lately I'm curious about my parents, and I don't know where to find an answer."

Ty paused, hoping to understand what she meant. "Are you curious about their marriage and what happened, or if they're your real parents, or—"

"I don't understand why they married. They were never a happy couple. I never heard a love phrase or saw any love in their actions. All I remember is their arguments. Maybe that's kept me from trusting marriage. It just seems to ruin things."

"Don't you have anyone that you can ask?"

"Grandma would have known, but I've waited too long to ask her."

He nodded, hearing a warning for his own delay and letting Mandy know how much he loved her.

She leaned her head on his shoulder. "I'd like to just walk away from this for a while and get my head together. Time is flying and—"

"Do you realize that plan makes sense?" Ty brushed his palm along her hair, enjoying the softness, yet wanting more. He longed to kiss her—a real kiss on the lips and not a peck on her cheek. "I've been doing a lot of thinking, Mandy, and I'd like to talk about it, but I don't want the tension we've had lately so I'll keep my mouth shut."

"No, don't, Ty. Please tell me what you're thinking."

She tilted her head to look into his eyes, but all he could focus on were her rosy lips. "Can you take a break today. We could go to the park and breathe fresh air and go over a timeline and what still needs to be done. If you need me, Mandy, I'm happy to help you. I know you want to get back to Chicago, and—"

"The more I'm determined, the more I face reality. I doubt if I can get done before the holidays, so I need to call the office, and...I don't know, Ty. I'm very confused."

"You've been through a difficult time. I know you loved your grandma, and you love your work and you're good at it. I really think your company will give you more time and let you work from here or even give you Bereavement time. Many companies have it for their employees."

"I suppose they do. It makes sense. I didn't ask for that much time, because I didn't know about the will, and I definitely didn't know all the things I had to handle."

"Call them. Then you'll know, and you'll feel better and stronger knowing where things stand."

For the first time that day, Mandy relaxed, and a smile eased her taut face. "I feel better already, Ty. Thank you. You always have the answers."

"We make a good team. You have the questions and I have the answers." He gave her a wink. "So, with that thought in mind, let's get some fresh air."

She gazed around the room, knowing she still had

lots to do, but she also needed free time. "I'll grab a sweater." She looked in the coat closet and found her sweater. Ty approached her, held out his hand and she grasped it. He gave it a squeeze as he opened the door and they stepped out into a perfect autumn day with colors that took her breath away.

♥

Ty pulled into Seven Lakes Park and found a spot in the shade. "Let's find a trail that heads down to the lake. It's late in the season so I'm guessing they don't have boat rentals this time of year."

"I'm happy to walk, Ty. I've been painting and working at the house for so many hours, I haven't noticed the autumn leaves, and they are beautiful. Orange, gold, coral. Really inspiring. It makes me realize what I'm missing in Chicago. I'm pretty much in the metro area of the city. There's only a few trees and not all of them have these gorgeous colors."

"Then I'm glad we came." He opened his door and headed for the passenger side. Mandy had already pushed her door open, so his hope of being a gentleman faded. Still he had time to clasp her hand as she stepped from the car. "Any place you'd like to walk?"

She pointed to the right. "We can follow the lake from here and I know there are some benches that way."

He didn't respond since he liked the bench idea. That could give them time to talk and find answers to Mandy's concerns. He knew she had some. As she stepped in that direction, he moved beside her. When their hands bumped, he slipped her hand in his, and he was pleased to see her smile.

"This is a great idea, Ty. I needed a break and this one is perfect. "Look ahead at the trees. They're beautiful. I'd almost forgotten autumn had come."

"Not only has it come, but in a few more weeks, winter will be here, so I have a few surprises up my sleeve."

She paused and studied the bottom of his arm. "Which sleeve?"

He laughed with her unexpected comment. "Not admitting a thing. You'll have to wait and see."

She shook her head and pulled him along into the wooded trail.

The scent of moist earth, pine, cedar, and dried leaves filled the air and looking up, the sunlight filtered through the golden leaves and warmed his soul with memories. Mandy and him walking to school together, laughing at silly things that happened during the day and then complaining about their homework.

"Ty, go that way." Mandy pointed toward a path he hadn't noticed. "I think there are a couple of benches down that way."

She wanted a bench for some reason, and he hated to ask. He followed her advice, and when they stepped past some underbrush, he found the path. Ty drew in a lengthy breath, aware of autumn in all its glory. "I can smell the special scents of this time of year."

"So can I. It is special. All we need are pumpkins."

He grinned to himself, aware of his plan, but he didn't want to give it away. "You mean pumpkin pies?"

"No. Plain old pumpkins."

"I'll see what I can do."

"Is that up your sleeve?" She gave him a sly grin as she glanced down his arm.

"I'm admitting nothing." He suspected what would happen next, and he'd been right. Mandy gave him a playful punch and put her nose in the air.

"Wonderful. She's baack!"

Mandy burst into laughter. "Like old times, Ty. And it feels good."

It felt too good to him. He longed to hold her in his arms, to breathe in the scent of her shampoo, and to feel the softness of her skin. "Those days were good, Mandy, and they don't have to be over."

Her smile faded. "It's good right now, but one of these days, Ty, I'm going to…"

"You don't have to tell me. I know all too well." He squeezed her hand and hoped she'd drop the subject of her life in Chicago. And nothing would happen unless he had the courage to tell her how much he cared for her. He'd waited too long. He had lost his courage and with so much time passing, he feared he would never find the nerve to be open and brave again.

Mandy broke loose from his hand and darted ahead of him. "You're too slow. Get a move on."

Her chuckle reached him and he sprinted through the trees, his eyes shifting from right to left, but somehow in that short time, he'd lost her. "Mandy, where are you?"

Only silence and bird calls answered him. He picked up his steps and ended up running down the rooted path until finally it opened up to the lake. He studied the glinting waves touched by the sun, rolled to shore as if sprinkled with silver and gold. He stepped closer to the beach, and finally spotted the bench she'd mentioned.

Mandy waved, a smile glowing on her face, but he couldn't smile back. She'd worried him when she'd seemed to vanish.

He headed down the beach, amazed that she'd gotten so far ahead of him. "Did you run?" He settled on the bench beside her.

"Not exactly, I know a short cut, and I walked fast. You were right, Ty. I needed to get out from under the paint and worry. It's great out here in the breeze off the lake. And look how beautiful it is."

"I noticed." He'd noticed she looked beautiful too. "You worried me. Did you know that?"

"Worried you? Why?"

"You could have gotten lost or tripped over one of the roots and fallen. How did I know?"

"Sorry, I suppose you didn't know, but I'm a big girl and can find my way."

His heart skipped when he heard her mention finding her way. "And that reminds me. I have a place I'd like to take you. It will be fun, and I think you'll find your pumpkin patch there."

"Really?" Her eyes widened. "Where is it?"

"That's one of the things up my sleeve."

She grinned. "That sleeve of yours must be loaded with secrets."

"But secrets I'll willingly share with you."

"But what about the house?"

"The house is as done as it needs to be. When we go back, if I can help you find the mementos and things you want to save, I can do that. The house has an attic, I think, and I'll climb the ladder and see what's up there."

"I want to do all of that before my mother comes.

From what she said, she'll be here in four or five days. That means working fast."

"Two of us can do it, Mandy. I have my Christmas order in, and so I can spare a few days from the store. We can do it together.

She shifted closer and rested her head on his shoulder. "You are so good to me, Ty, so good I feel guilty."

"Guilty? For what?" He had her cornered. "Then that means you owe me something, right?"

"That depends." She grinned. "We'll have to discuss that."

He nodded and managed to hold back his grin. The more playful they were, the more he sensed he could tell her how long he'd had stronger feelings for her than she realized. Still he hated taking a chance that could ruin everything."

"Here's an idea, let's take care of the house tonight. You know, finding the things you want to keep, and then tomorrow, I'll pull one of those secrets out of my sleeve. How's that?"

"It better be something special, since you've aroused my curiosity more than once today."

"It's special." He slipped his arm around her shoulders and gave her a hug. "You'll thank me afterward."

"Okay, I'm counting on it."

"I'm counting on you, my dear. We'll have some silly fun like the old days."

She turned sideways, his arm still around her shoulder, and gazed at him as if looking for something special. "I loved the old days, but I suppose it's time for some new days to add to them."

New days? Ty's head spun guessing what she meant. Was she looking for more than friendship? He was and had been for too long. He tripped over his tongue, trying to form words. "That sounds good, Mandy. I look forward to new things, especially unexpected new things."

"Or secrets. I know you have a sleeve full of them."

He chuckled "Tomorrow, I'll get rid of a couple of those secrets, at least."

"I can't wait." She slipped her hand over his and gave it a squeeze. "So, if all this is happening, we'd better get going. We still have to deal with tonight and the mementos I'd like to keep."

"Right?" He stood and clasped her hand to help her rise.

She faced him, her eyes searching his. "You're a gem, Ty. No wonder I miss you so much when we're not together."

Fighting his longing to kiss her, Ty, gazed into her lovely blue eyes, "Let's solve that problem. Maybe we should spend more time together. What do you think?"

Mandy focused on the sky before looking at him. "I think we'd have to live in the same city. That's pretty much impossible, don't you think?"

"I'd have to sell my store, but it's something to think about."

Mandy remained silent as if searching for a response. "Right. Or in my case, not without changing my job or…" She raised her eyes to his. "Or do what I do right now, make a deal to work at home and go to Chicago for occasional meetings."

Ty's heart thunder against his chest. "Good plan, my love. Let's give this some thought."

♥

Mandy's mind tumbled with what she'd said about remaining in Holly. Though it had always seemed impossible, today she asked herself why. Fixing the problem had slipped from her mouth as easy as skates on ice. She only had to do what she was already doing. And she would never want Ty to give up his hardware store. That was his life's work, and a huge investment. Apparently, he made a good living owning the store, and she'd heard people say he was a smart man and ran a good store.

Yet had they both been serious about wanting to be together? Theirs was a friendship, not a romance, and yet they'd been as close as any romance, except they were missing the outward signs of love. She'd kissed him on the cheek a week or so earlier and it surprised her. In fact, she eyed his shapely lips for a moment, but the idea of kissing his lips made her uncomfortable. She knew Ty only wanted a friendship and lately thinking about her mother and father's bad marriage, it dawned on her that she too might use that fear to stop her from looking at anyone seriously. Nothing made sense.

Mandy set another of her grandmother's photo albums into the box Ty had brought from the store, and pulled her thoughts back to the job of gathering mementos and things she wanted to keep. She heard Ty's voice but couldn't make out what he said.

"What?" She rose and headed for the dining room where she'd last seen him.

Ty stood in front of her grandmother's buffet holding a plate. "Have you seen these dishes?" He held one up so she could see it."

"I don't think so." She walked toward him, eyeing the white plate rimmed with a golden design woven around bunches of Forget Me Nots. "It's beautiful, Ty. I wonder why grandma didn't use them. I'm quite sure she never put them on the table for any holiday dinners or for company. I was here a few times when she had guests. She used a standard set of white dishes with a brown rim. They were okay, but not beautiful."

Ty handed her the plate and she turned it over and read the emblem on the back. "It's Royal Doulton, Ty. How many dishes are there?"

"They're on the shelves down here. Take a look." He opened the door, and she leaned over to look inside. "Wow. It looks like a whole set, ten or twelve dinner plates, dessert plates, salad bowls, cups and saucers plus some serving dishes, a platter, two serving bowls, and more." She lifted one of the coffee cups and studied it. "I would love to have this set, Ty. They're beautiful and perfect for a dinner party."

"They're yours, Mandy. I'll pick up a box made for chinaware so the pieces will be protected."

"Thanks, Ty. I've packed all the albums. I'll look at them later, and I found a few curios I would like to keep. Everything else my mother and the cousins can have." She faltered. "But now I have to move the china and this stuff out of the house or they'll be missing. The only place I can think of to put them is my car."

"Mandy, I have a house. I'll take them there tonight, and the boxes will be safe there."

"Thanks, Ty. I seem to look for the worst solution instead of the better."

Ty moved closer to her and drew her into his arms. "Mandy, you are under a lot of pressure, some you've caused yourself. But no matter, you are bound to be tense and stressed. You're dealing with too many issues that need resolving."

"You always understand, Ty. Always." She rested her head on his shoulder. "I'm exhausted. Let's stop for now. I think we've found everything I would want to keep, and I'll leave the rest for the cousins and my mother, if she even wants anything. Are you hungry?"

"Starving." He brushed her hair from her cheek. "In fact, I think I heard your stomach rumble."

"So did I." She grinned. "Order pizza or go somewhere?"

"Let's go the The Villagers' Family Restaurant. Great meatloaf and chicken."

"Sounds great, and then I'm going to bed. I'm exhausted."

"Stress does that, my love. Get a good rest tonight. Tomorrow we take a break, and you'll get to see your pumpkin patch."

"And?" She nestled closer.

"And?" He drew back to look into her face. "Give me a hint."

"I think it's up your sleeve."

He chuckled. His sleeve had a lot of action lately, and he loved it. "Right. I will reveal one secret in the sleeve. But before you fall asleep standing up, let's eat."

"Right." She straightened her back and headed for the door.

Chapter 7

Ty awoke, eager to get going. He'd planned a fun day that he hoped would distract her from her mother's visit and all the other stresses she seemed to struggle with. Problems even more than he could number and yet he understood her plight. Soon her almost estranged mother was to visit, and yet, he knew that the visit most likely had to do with the inheritance Mandy had received from her grandmother's estate—her father's mother—and nothing to do with Mandy's mother.

He turned and looked at his face in his bedroom mirror and wished he hadn't. Sleep did evade him more than usual during the night, and today he realized Mandy's stresses were causing him grief too.

Though he'd planned a fun day, even fun wouldn't help Mandy resolve the tension she was to face. He longed to have answers that would give her assistance, since she often depended on him to help solve her problems or at least, provide steps to a solution.

He covered his yawn and sat on the edge of the bed. Today he needed a plan, but nothing came to mind.

Would staying out of her problem be the best way to help her? One day, Mandy would vanish from his life and have to face everything on her own, unless she fell in love with a man who was a good problem solver. The thought struck his chest harder than a sledgehammer.

Would he ever be able to walk away before he faced the opposite and watched her walk away?

Pushing himself from the mattress, Ty stood a moment and shook his head, hoping to chase away the thoughts clashing in his mind. He stomped his foot like an angry child and grew angrier at the ridiculous drama.

"Stop." Startled by his bellow, he grabbed his shoes and headed for the kitchen. He'd eat and get going, but when he opened the refrigerator, food turned his stomach. His actions turned it worse, and he knew change had to happen. He could be a friend to Mandy but not the dear friend he'd been. No matter how hard he tried to see their friendship, he only saw a deception. He'd fallen in love while Mandy clung to their friendship. It couldn't be. Not if he wanted to respect himself, and that was questionable.

His big up-his-sleeve surprise had lost its purpose and the fun he'd anticipated. Yet, he didn't want to add another disappointment or negative situation to Mandy's life. She had too much going on to let her down.

He checked the weather, slipped on a lightweight jacket and headed out the door. He could handle the day since he'd made a big deal out of it. He hoped he could.

♥

Mandy heard a car pull into the driveway, and she prayed it was Ty. She hurried to the window as relief spread through her. He saw her because he gave her a wave and she sent one back. When she opened the door, Ty stood there with a faint grin, but one that looked stressed. Though tempted to ask if something was wrong, she ignored it. He would tell her without being asked.

"Ready?"

She looked down at her slacks and shoes. "Am I dressed right? I have no idea where we're going."

"You look perfect. Just bring along a light jacket. Just in case."

His just-in-case made her curious. The sky was blue, and the weather forecast sounded like a typical autumn. She opened the coat closet and pulled out a warm cardigan that would keep out a chill if necessary. She tossed it over her arm and reached for her shoulder bag.

"You don't need to lug that, or we can lock it in the car if you think you'll need something."

"Money to buy a pumpkin." She grinned.

This time his expression joined his grin. "I can afford a pumpkin."

"If you say so." She elbowed him with a chuckle. "Then let's go."

He didn't respond but turned to the door and held it open for her.

Mandy stepped outside as an odd feeling whirled in her chest. Ty's grins and comments seemed stressed, and she sensed he was concerned about her problems as he so often did. He came to her aid more than his own needs, and she began to think Ty didn't have time to do things for himself. But today wasn't the day to resolve it.

He opened the car door while she slipped in, and he rounded the car to the driver's seat. He plopped onto the seat and started the car without a word. So different than usual. And even more strange, Ty turned on the radio, upped the volume, and pulled away again in silence.

As they drove along the highway, she tried to guess where they were going, but her thoughts kept heading back to the strain she sensed from Ty's behavior. Though he'd seemed enthusiastic about this fun day he'd planned, his attitude felt more like heading to a funeral. Not wanting to ask, she remained silent as well, praying that something would change the tense atmosphere.

Tired of the silence, Mandy turned down the radio volume and turned to face Ty. "Obviously something is wrong, Ty, and if this is a bad day, we can forget the fun day.

"Sorry, Mandy. I have lots on my mind. Nothing I want to talk about right now. Anyway, we're almost there."

"We're in farmland, so I suppose this is where we'll find the pumpkin patch."

He nodded, but then glanced her way. "That and more."

"More?" Mandy studied his face.

"You'll see. We're close."

She closed her mouth, not wanting to ruin his surprise with her questions. But she had many questions today. Questions that concerned her. What happened to her talkative and playful long-time friend?"

In moments, Ty turned into a long wide driveway where a sign read: Bonadeo Farms.

She'd never heard of the place before, but then she had no reason too. She'd been a big city girl and farms had never been an interest, although today, this one was.

As Ty pulled further down the driveway, she spotted cars parked on the edge of a field and some outbuildings, a large barn and some sheds and what looked like a house. Her curiosity rose, but she waited, not wanting to deal with Ty's silence.

He pulled into the line of cars, jumped out and opened her door.

Mandy stepped out as she gazed around at the buildings and noticed a large corn field with people heading into the corn. Finally, it dawned on her. "It's a corn maze. I've never walked through one of those."

"This one is different from what I've heard." Ty shrugged. "I'm not sure what that means."

"I guess we'll find out." She reached for her sweater and then changed her mind.

Ty rested his hand against her back. "Let's go and see what we have in store."

To Mandy, seeing what's in store wasn't as meaningful as learning what was troubling Ty. She clamped her jaw together to help her remember not to question him about anything.

They stopped at a visitor stand and were given rules for the corn maze. As she read, she faltered and stopped to share it with Ty. "Did you know that the house over there..." She pointed to the building. "Is part of the corn maze."

Ty nodded. "I did. It's connected somehow with the corn maze?"

"But did you know it's a 'supposed' haunted

house?" Mandy gazed ahead staring at the innocent looking white house. She didn't believe in haunted, but she got the idea. The visitor would have to face the unexpected. But then, the whole tone of the trip had been unexpected.

"I heard that too, and that's one of the surprises."

Mandy stared at him. "One of those up your sleeve?"

"No, but I do have another one up my sleeve." He grinned, and his expression relaxed her. Ty, for some wonderful reason, had become his old self.

"Share the secret, Ty." She shifted closer to him, happy to see his familiar levity.

"Okay. Are you ready?"

She gave a quick nod.

"As we weave our way through the maze, we have to be on the lookout."

"Lookout? Don't tell me for ghosts or vampires."

Ty out and out laughed. "Probably that too, but look for a small red ribbon. Whoever finds one receives a gift."

"What kind of gift? Mandy narrowed her eyes, searching his face for a hint. She figured it would be something ridiculous.

"Something you've wanted, Mandy. A free pumpkin."

"Really." Her pitch rose to a squeal.

"Really, and you can select it, so it will be exactly what you want." Ty gave her another smile.

Her heart leaped with relief and happiness. This was the Ty she'd known so long. "I'll let you cut it into any kind of face you want, Ty."

"Really? Hm? I'll see if I can carve your face. No

clowns, cats or monsters. Just a lovely woman anxious for a carved pumpkin."

She loved hearing him call her lovely. The past few days he'd drifted away from her. Today he'd come back. "Thank you, Ty. Maybe we can carve two and I'll make a handsome man with black hair and eyes the color of the sky."

"I don't know anyone who looks like that." Ty looked away, noticing the crowd was thinning down. "We should get going. Look." He pointed to the thinning crowd. "We can whip through that maze in a minute."

Mandy tried to roll her eyes. "You really think so?" She gazed again at the long stretch of corn stalks. "I'll say we can't, and if I'm right you owe me something special. I'll decide what."

"You'll decide. Okay, I'll take you up on that."

For the first time that day, Ty grasped her hand and led her to the entrance of the maze. Her spirit lifted higher than it had in days. Even though her mother was coming, it didn't dampen her happiness.

She stayed close to Ty, realizing within minutes that some turns in the maze where dead ends and even though some appeared to lead somewhere, the path didn't. She assigned herself the job of looking for the red ribbon, and she thought the search would distract her from the occasional ghost face peaking at her through the corn stalks.

Ty laughed when she jumped and let out a shriek, but he clung to her hand as if he understood she needed reassurance. "Try to be prepared for things to happen in the maze. It won't scare you as much."

"Great idea, but it's not working. I'm concentrating

on the red ribbon, and I've failed."

He pressed his lips together, trying not to laugh. He couldn't fool her, since it was not a laughing matter.

"Ty, I realize this is a game, and I know something's going to happen, but I think I make it worse by anticipating it."

Ty gave her hand a squeeze. "We'll be through the maze soon, and then we just have the house."

"Haunted house, remember?"

He looked away, again, trying to muzzle a laugh. "I know this is silly to you, but not to me."

"Don't forget it's a good distraction. You've been working so hard to get that house ready, and you need a break from all of that."

His tender expression touched her. "And my mother's visit. That's harder than painting every wall in that house."

"Why, Mandy? I know she's been distant, but I'm sure she has a reason. Have you talked with her about it?"

"Talked? My mother won't budge on talking about much of anything, Ty. You should remember that from our school days."

His head drooped while he focused on the straw covered path. "I suppose I should remember, but I apparently forgot. I'm sorry."

"Let's drop it, Ty. I'm focusing on a red ribbon. You focus on getting me out of here."

This time he laughed. "Let's get moving then."

He picked up the pace and walked so fast she feared she would miss the red ribbon.

After a few more ghost faces peeked at them and wrong turns that caused them to head back to correct their mistake, Ty saw the end of the maze.

Mandy took a deep breath, pleased that she'd survived the ghosts and goblins, but she still hadn't spotted the ribbon. "Ty, I didn't find—"

"Hold on my love." He tightened the grip on her hand and hurried her toward the end of the maze.

"Ty, you don't understand, I really want—"

"We can buy a pumpkin, but don't—"

"But the fun is to get it free. I really wanted to find a ribbon."

"You will."

She stopped while he kept going, stretching her arm as far as he could. "Okay, Ty. I give up."

"Good." He continued to pull her to the end of the maze. "Now look."

Look? She saw the haunted house ahead of her, but Ty wasn't looking that way. She stared ahead, her eyes shifting from the top of the corn stalks to the right and left, and then she looked down. A flash of red caught her eye.

"It's down there." She pointed to an ear of corn decorated with a red ribbon. She pulled it off and dangled it in Ty's face. "Got it."

♥

Ty eyed the red ribbon that had caused so much drama. "Congratulations. Now we can enjoy ourselves without whining."

"Whining?" She gave him a playful punch. "You're just jealous that I found it."

"I am. You're right." He laughed at the ridiculous search for a silly ribbon. "But I'll tell you something. I knew you would find it."

"You did?"

"First, you're determined, although I call it stubborn, and you're decisive. You have the ability to get what you want." As the words left him, he sensed a deeper meaning to his statement. He'd hoped for the past few years that Mandy would return to Holly and realize she needed him forever.

"Thank you, Ty. I'm taking that as a compliment." She shifted closer, raised herself on tiptoes and kissed his forehead. He struggled not to shift his head so her kiss would reach his mouth.

Mandy didn't move, but gazed up at him, her eyes searching his, and he longed to know what she was thinking. "You're the best, Ty. I've never met another man like you."

Though he tried to move or speak, Ty couldn't. He needed to act, to say something, to open his heart and tell her the truth. Yet the cowardice that kept him silent took over his senses. Fighting his silence, he knew what he had to say. "I've never met a woman like you, Mandy. Never."

"Is that good or bad, Ty?"

"Ask yourself the same question, and you'll have the answer."

Though she looked confused, he could picture her tossing the question around in her mind.

"I suppose it's how you look at it, Ty. Does that make sense?"

"Perfect sense. Now let's get out of here and get your free pumpkin before the best ones are gone."

She came back to life. "Right. Let's go." She grasped his hand, and they hurried back toward the pumpkin patch and Ty's car.

Once Mandy picked out her pumpkin, Ty bought one too. He'd joked about carving a pumpkin to look like her, and he needed a pumpkin to at least try. Once in the car, he drove them over to the building away from the pumpkins and stopped.

Mandy's headed pivoted his way. "What are you doing?"

"Be patient. It's one final surprise."

He opened the driver's door and hurried around the car to open her door. The first thing she said made him laugh. "It's that sleeve of yours again isn't it?"

"You guessed it. That thing is packed full." He drew her toward him. "This won't take long." He grasped her hand and led her to the building. When he opened the door, the sweet scent filled the air.

Mandy faltered and gazed up at him. "Cider. I love it."

"I know, but take another deep breath."

She jumped and wrapped her arms around his neck. "And donuts."

"Fresh donuts. They make them here."

He didn't have to invite her inside. She darted into the building as he followed, chuckling at her new enthusiasm. He remembered the many times in autumn they'd gone to the cider mill.

"Ty, this brings back wonderful memories."

He nodded. "Let's make some new ones."

He heard no argument from Mandy. He purchased a large jug of cider and a box of donuts. As soon as they returned to the car, Mandy dug in the box, and they sat in the car eating the still warm donuts. The only thing they missed was the cider.

When Mandy finished the donut, she sat a moment

in silence before reaching over for Ty's hand. "Thank you so much for the great treat and especially for the distraction. You know my mind is stuck on what's to come." She looked his way. "And that's my mother."

"Mandy, you don't have to thank me for—"

"Ty, those are the sweet things you've done for me all my life. You know when I need to be distracted and when I need to be calmed or need an answer. You just seem to know."

"You do the same, Mandy." Ty pressed her hand. "You don't realize how often you helped me with a problem or situation without knowing it."

She lowered her head. "I wish I could do more."

"You do enough. Instead of reminiscing the past, let's work on the future. We have pumpkins to carve."

A laugh shot from her and surprised him.

"That was scary, Ty. You're sounding too much like me."

He winked. "That's a good thing, isn't it?" He pointed to the two pumpkins. "And now to carve."

♥

Mandy hurried into her grandmother's house and set her carved pumpkin on a table by the front window and then plopped onto the loveseat while her head spun. Her mother said she would arrive soon, but gave no specifics which left Mandy hanging off a cliff. But why was she surprised? Her mother's life was to do what she wanted without considering the impact on others.

A ragged breath rattled through Mandy's chest. If only she had come from a family like Ty's. His parents were wonderful. They all cared about each other and supported each other. If she ever married, that's the kind of family she longed for—a family filled with love. Ty had been blessed.

She forced the yearning out of her mind and faced reality. She needed to get ready for her mother's visit, whenever that would be. The house looked as good as it was going to get. She and Ty had painted and then packed away the items she wanted to keep—the lovely China, a few curios, and the photo albums. But what her mother might want was the big question, and she wouldn't know for sure until she arrived.

Her best guess was money. Her mother and the cousins tended to ride the same road. Money. Grandma had a savings but not a fortune by any means. She had two investments, but taking the money out would be unwise. Her available savings was the kind people kept for a rainy day. Though the sun shined through the window, she feared the rainy day might be closer than she wanted.

Ty's offer to take home the items she wanted to keep, and as always, he'd saved the day. At least she didn't have to fight for the things that meant the most to her. Meant the most. The phrase boiled in her chest. What had her mother ever done for her father's mother. Nothing but cause sorrow. She'd walked out on them too often. What kind of person returned home when they ran out of money and stuck around until they could wheedle enough money to eventually leave again?

Tears blurred her eyes, and she swiped them away, frustrated at her emotional reaction to something she'd lived with for too long. Ty had been her rescuer when he suspected problems, and eventually getting away to Chicago had saved her.

She slapped her hand on the loveseat's arm.

"Enough." She marched across the room, surveyed what changes she and Ty had made and nodded. Everything looked neat and cozy. That made the house saleable or livable.

Livable? The past few weeks, she found herself more and more picturing herself living in her grandmother's house. The neighbors made her comfortable, and—once again, Lauren came into her thoughts. She liked Ty, and he liked her. Or were their feelings stronger? Her chest tightened, and the warning riled her. She'd talked with Ty about not having lady friends. She bugged him about finding someone and getting married.

What did she really want? Losing Ty would break her heart, and as much as she denied it, the truth needed to be faced. Had their friendship grown to something deeper? Truth? She feared it had, at least for her. She longed to kiss him the way lovers kissed and not the little peck on his cheek.

Mandy jumped, hearing a knock on the door. Her mother already. She closed her eyes and prayed that she could get through the visit without falling apart. Before she pulled herself together, the door opened and when she looked, relief washed over h her. "Ty, it's you. I thought it—"

"Sorry, Mandy. I should have remembered you're expecting your mother." He went to her and drew her into his arms. "You've been on my mind all day."

"You're always on mine. One day, we should—"

A hard double knock stopped them both. Mandy's lungs emptied as panic knotted her chest. "It's her."

Ty backed toward the kitchen. "I'll leave through the back, Mandy. Hang in there."

His expression twisted her heart as she pressed her lips together longing to beg him to stay, but Ty was right. She needed to be alone.

Drawing herself up, her back straightened as she dug for courage and control. "Coming." She put on a brave face and opened the door. "Hello, mother."

"Amanda, it's good to see you."

All Mandy managed was a nod. "Come in."

Her mother paused before she grasped the door frame and pushed herself into the room. "It's been a long time."

"Yes, years." Mandy motioned toward a chair. "Have a seat."

Again, her mother gazed around the room before stepping forward. "I suppose you're surprised that I decided to visit you."

"Not really, mother. When grandma died, I assumed the cousins let you know. They were here evaluating the worth of the house and furnishings."

"Really? I suppose they want to buy the house."

"Buy? No. They want me to give them whatever they think is of value. The problem is this, I haven't had a minute to talk with a realtor, nor have I decided to sell the house."

From her mother's expression, Mandy couldn't decide if she were surprised, curious, or angry.

"Are you planning to live here? I thought you worked out of state."

"I do, but most of my work can be done at home, so it is possible to live here. I haven't made any decisions."

"Do you think that's fair to your grandmother's family? You've made all these decisions on your own?

What about a will?"

"Grandma's will left everything to her nearest relative. No one else was included, and no other directives."

"I suppose I'm one of her closest—"

"You? Mother, you were an in-law." Mandy caught her breath. "I'm surprised you even considered yourself related to grandma. You never saw her or did anything for her. She was daddy's mother. I don't think you got along with her."

"Well, a will has to be legal or it can be challenged."

Mandy controlled something building in her chest. Either a scream or a laugh, "The will is legal. Dena and Gwen also tried to challenge it, and their argument was knocked down by grandma's lawyer. Sorry, mother, but none of the property belongs to you. If this is why you came, you wasted your time."

"I don't like your attitude, Amanda. Is it wrong that I came to visit you?'

"It's not wrong. It's a surprise. I haven't seen you for years. The same with Gwen and Dena."

"I didn't think it was a sin to visit your own daughter."

Mandy struggled to breathe. "No sin. Just a coincidence. Both you and the cousins, happened to come when grandma died and left a will."

Her mother's expression said all she needed to see. "If you'd like a memento of grandma's to remember her, I have a few things around the house that you're welcome to take."

"A memento? That's rather generous."

The sarcasm wasn't lost, but Mandy didn't let it

stop her. "It's the right thing to do. I put a few things away for grandma's neighbors. Some of them were very close to her. You probably remember Edith, for one."

"Edith. You're giving something to Edith?"

"She spent hours and hours helping with the funeral gathering, preparing food, welcoming the guests, and cleaning up. She and grandma were close. Why wouldn't I offer her something of grandma's?"

"I suppose your grandmother left a savings. Are you sharing the money with the neighbors?"

Mandy had to hold her breath rather than speak. Her mother sounded like the cousins.

"Mother, how often did you visit grandma? Can you recall what you did for her out of kindness? I could sit here and make a list of things Edith did for grandma. For one, she stopped by daily to see if grandma needed anything? Even I didn't do that."

Her mother's jaw dropped as if she wanted to respond, but she seemed at a loss for words.

"Let's end this conversation. It's going to get us nowhere. As you wander through the house, let me know if you see anything you'd like of grandma's, and you're welcome to have it."

"You said that, but are you selling the house?

"I don't know. I told you that earlier. I need to speak with a realtor, and since the house is mine, I'm giving thought to keeping it."

"Keep it?" Her mother's tone pierced her ears. "Is that in the will, Amanda? Did your grandmother not think of anyone else?"

"The will left everything to me. I told you that and remember that grandma is daddy's mother. I'm her only living relative. You were an in-law."

Her mother leaned forward, her face flushed.

"Speaking of daddy. Why did you marry him? You and daddy were never happy together. You both seemed so uncomfortable with each other. I never saw you hold hands or hug or kiss. I can't understand what caused you to marry."

"Amanda, first of all your father's and my marriage has nothing to do with you. Not every parent kisses and hugs in front of their children. You don't know how we acted when you weren't there so stop judging me and your father."

"I'm not judging. I'm trying to understand. You know, mother, I have not considered marriage, because I want one based on love and companionship. How do I know that mine will be like that? You and dad must have had some expectation when you married, and I wish I knew if you were disappointed in your marriage or if that's what you both wanted. Distance."

"Distance? What does that mean? As I already told you, we were fine. We just didn't display our relationship in front of you."

"I'm sorry you didn't show affection. Maybe I wouldn't be as concerned for my own relationships. When I visit Ty's family, family love is evident. They're not hugging and kissing but there's laughter and joy when I'm with them. They are comfortable together and—"

"Maybe they'll adopt you, Amanda, although you're a bit old for that."

"I'm sorry, Mother. I'm not trying to insult you or judge you."

"Really?" Her mother's sarcastic pitch felt like a

slap.

"I'm trying to understand. I want a marriage that is loving and filled with caring, but I'm trying to understand, since I would think you and dad wanted the same thing, and—"

"Amanda, don't try to guess what your father and I wanted. People are different. You can't compare us to Ty's family. So stop trying. Don't you think I have expectations? Since you're the heir of your grandmother's home and savings, I would anticipate being included. I'm tired of your grilling, Amanda. And I had no idea you were so selfish."

Mandy slammed her mouth closed. If she were selfish, she'd learned selfishness from her mother, but saying it would only rile her more. "Dena and Gwen thought I'd done some 'hanky panky' on the will, so I gave them the name of the lawyer who drew up grandma's will." She walked to a drawer in one of her lamp tables and pulled out the attorney's business card. "Here you go." She handed her mother a business card. I know we'll both be happy if you check with him. He will answer all your questions. I had nothing to do with grandma's will."

Her mother eyed the business card, and then gave her a questioning look. "Is this your attorney?"

"I don't have an attorney. He was grandma's lawyer. I'm sure he will answer any question you have. I only saw him at the reading of the will. That's when he gave me his business cards."

Her mother eyed the cards, turning them over and back again as if she were looking for a flaw or a sign that the card had been tampered with. Mandy didn't want to end her visit on a bad note, but the situation had become very unpleasant. No matter what she said, her mother studied her as if scrutinizing her every move and word. She began to feel guilty for no reason.

"I suppose I should go and leave you with your inheritance and overt gloating."

Mandy clamped her jaw so tight it ached. She'd had enough of the guilt and drama caused by something lovely, her grandmother's thoughtful gift to her because she loved her, and Mandy loved her grandmother.

"Mother, I'm not gloating, but I'll never convince you of that. I was as shocked as you are that grandma left everything to me. I am her only living family not including in-laws, and that's the only reason I can think of as to why she chose me. I loved grandma and visited her as often as I could. I know she appreciated my visits. She was sometimes very lonely."

"Again, I'm leaving, and I will talk to this questionable attorney. You may hear from me again."

"Before you go, would you like to look at some of the mementos that you might want,"

Her mother appeared to roll her eyes. "You can forget the mementos. I'll be back for something of value. Something like a share of the house's value when you sell it."

"I haven't decided that yet, as I told you. I'm thinking about staying in Holly and living here."

Her mother arched her brows and snorted. "Well, good luck. I really need to leave."

"Have a safe trip wherever you're going, Mother. If you'd like to stay connected, you could give me your address or phone number."

"Goodbye, Amanda. Perhaps I will see you again. Maybe sooner than you think." She turned and headed to the door without further comment. When she flung the door open, she didn't look back, and darted outside to her car.

"Goodbye, Mother. Have a safe trip." Mandy spoke to herself, but no matter what she said, she suspected it would be twisted into something negative."

Chapter 8

Ty hurried to the door, concerned how Mandy handled her mother's visit. In the confusion, that morning, he realized that Thanksgiving was in three days. He guessed Mandy hadn't remembered either.

When he opened the door, he listened and heard noise coming from somewhere in the house. "Mandy?" He moved between the living room and the dining room and waited.

"Ty? Is that you. I'm in the kitchen."

He turned in that direction and found her sitting on the floor with piles of dishes, pots and pans, bowls, and everything he could imagine. "What are you doing?"

"I've made a decision, and that motivated me to put the kitchenware and dishes in a logical place so I can find what I need."

"Good idea." His chest tightened, guessing what her decision had been. "Tell me, what's your decision?" He held his breath.

"I'm going to stay here in grandma's house for three months or maybe four and see how it works out with my job. I posed the idea and the honcho's approved. They know I do much of my work now in that type of situation."

He slipped his arm around her. "Great plan. Testing it is good, and then you have options. While living here, I can help you make any other changes you still want done. You know I don't mind at all."

"I can't keep letting you do all of this free, Ty. I—"

"Well, my dear, I'm not letting you pay me or whatever your idea is, so get used to it."

"But—"

"No buts. You can help me when I need someone. For example, I have Thanksgiving reservations at Holly Hotel, and I need a date."

Her head snapped upward, her eyes shifting from him to the sky. "I forgot about Thanksgiving. I think it's next Thursday. It seems so long ago that you made the reservations."

"It was weeks ago, but if I'd waited until now, they'd be booked. That place is popular, plus while we're there, we can stand on the high porch or on the sidewalk and watch A Christmas Carol. They put on that play outside the hotel every year. Have you seen it?"

Mandy tilted her head skyward. "It's the one with Tiny Tim and Scrooge, right?"

He nodded. "Right. What do you say?"

"I say I'd love to see it."

"Great. It's a tradition I've enjoyed for years, and I hoped you'd like to see it too."

She grinned. "I enjoy traditions, new events, and surprises. Things up your sleeve."

"There you go again, sweetheart. You're always

after what's up there."

"And you know why?

Her question circled in his mind. "You like surprises."

She gave a shrug. "That's one reason. The other is I'm doing them with you." She tilted her head upward, and he waited for her to kiss his cheek as she sometimes did.

Instead, Ty's lungs emptied as she leaned closer and kissed his lips. He gasped, embarrassed that she probably heard him. "Thank you, kind lady." He wanted to sound casual, but his pitch had risen too far above normal, and he sounded as if he'd run a five-mile marathon.

Mandy's discomfort showed on her face. "I probably shouldn't have done that, Ty. I'm sorry that I shocked you."

"Shocked me? No not at all." When the words left him, he knew it was a lie and so did she. "Let me rephrase that. It was a pleasant…a very pleasant surprise. And one not up my sleeve."

She grinned, and he managed to smile also. Yet the sleeve reference gave him an idea. He could tuck another of those surprises up his sleeve, a pleasant surprise, he hoped.

On Thanksgiving afternoon, Ty and Mandy walked up the porch steps of the Holly Hotel, looking forward to the holiday in the special location. When they entered, a delicious scent filled the air, a blend of roasted turkey and braised pork.

Mandy pointed to one of the tables along the windows. "I'm really impressed by the table settings, Ty. They're perfection."

He nearly chuckled, but stopped himself. Though his interest was the food he would eat, he agreed that the pots of autumn plants and flowers—deep russet, orange and gold—in the center of the table was a perfect reflection of the season. Surrounding the floral display, the brown-toned tableware with brown and white linens, added to the autumn theme.

They were seated in a convenient location near a window so if their meal wasn't complete when The Christmas Carol players began, they could still watch the beginning from their seats.

Their soup arrived first, butternut squash with pumpkin butter and next the salad with harvest lettuce, spiced walnuts, chipped Derby cheese, local honey and cider. Besides the turkey and pork, they had the option to choose pan seared Michigan walleye, and even a vegetarian dish of autumn ratatouille with gruyere cheese.

"Ty, this is absolutely delicious. I've never had a meal so elegant and unusual."

"It's not a typical Thanksgiving dinner, but you're right. It's excellent." He had taken a peek at the desserts, and he was tempted to warn her to save room."

More customers had been seated, and a few had been guided to the historic bar in the next room to wait for seating. "Mandy, do you know the history of this hotel?"

Question filled her face as her brow wrinkled. "I may have been told, but I can't remember."

Ty waited a moment, hoping to stir her interest. He loved the story.

Mandy touched his hand. "Tell me about it, and this time I'll remember.

"I might not recall everything, but as far as I remember, the city had been chosen to have a train depot built right here in this area. So, once the tracks were down, the townsmen heard the clack of twenty-five trains making its way through the town bringing many visitors and no inns for the guest. So, in 1863, the hotel was built to accommodate the multitude of visitors."

Mandy gazed at him with her usual questioning squint. "It's interesting that a small town like this one had a depot. I would think they might have built one in a larger town."

"I'm sure they did, but I believe this was the first stretch of the tracks, so it makes sense. The other famous thing that happened here is that while prohibition was ending, many people, especially women, were against drinking, and Holly Hotel had the bar, the same one that's here now." He pointed to the doorway. "If we remember before we leave, you can go in and see it. There's a painting over the counter that was very opposed by the women, It's a scantily dressed woman, and between the painting and the alcohol, one of the great prohibitionists, Carrie Nation, arrived one day with a group of angry ladies who attacked the pub with umbrellas, threw whiskey bottles, while Carrie Nation came with a hatchet."

Mandy chuckled. "I'll have to take a look before we leave."

"And right now, we'd better eat this meal before we miss out on the dessert. Pumpkin pies with fresh cinnamon cream and Pecan bread pudding."

Mandy's eyes widened as he listed the choices.

"Ty, this is wonderful. I'm so glad you suggested

it."

"I'm glad, Mandy. I've always liked it here. Great food, lots of history, and it's known for its ghost inhabitants."

"What?" Mandy leaned back, her eyes shifting around the dining room. "You're kidding, right?"

"Not really. I've never seen a ghost, but I hear some people have."

"But I don't believe in ghosts." He rubbed his index finger along her hand now clutching his arm. "I'm sure they ignore those who don't believe."

"Wonderful, and thanks for warning me."

She turned her attention back to the meal, but occasionally, he caught her glancing this way and that as if making sure they were ghost-free.

While they enjoyed their dessert, Ty noticed the crowd growing outside the building, and surmised the play would begin soon. "See the crowd." He motioned toward the window. "The Christmas Carol is about to start."

"I'm full, Ty. The dessert is great, but I don't think I can eat another bite."

He nodded and beckoned to the waitress. In moments, she arrived with the bill. He handed her his credit card, and in a few minutes, they stepped outside in time to see the beginning of the play.

Ebenezer Scrooge sat in his counting-house Christmas Eve with his clerk Bob Cratchet shaking from the cold. Two gentlemen walk in, asking Scrooge for a donation to their charity which he refuses with venom. When the men wish him a Merry Christmas, as they leave, Scrooge yells Bah Humbug.

When Scrooge arrives home, he is visited by the

ghost of his former partner Jacob Marley, weighted heavy with chains, and he warns Scrooge if he doesn't change, things will get worse. For the next three nights, he will be visited by three spirits. Scrooge doesn't listen, but Marley appears again, weighted down with chains and tells Scrooge that he is punished for his greed and must wander the earth in chains as punishment. Scrooge doesn't listen and is awakened by the Ghost of Christmas Past who takes Scrooge on a journey through his past life.

Two more times, Scrooge is visited by a spirit. The next is The Ghost of Christmas Present where he observes a family struggling to find enough food for their Christmas dinner, and he recognizes his clerk Bob Cratchet and his crippled son, Tiny Tim. He sees their happiness and begs the spirit to let him stay and enjoy the party.

The third evening, The Ghost of Christmas Yet To Come appears and Scrooge listens to people discussing a dead man who was a creditor and their happiness that he died. When Scrooge sees the headstone, he is shocked to see his name. He begs the spirit for another chance and promises to change and share his wealth and to honor Christmas with all his heart. He sees Tiny Tim and greats him with love and kindness. He provides lavish gifts for the poor around him and enjoys the generosity that he shares with others. As years pass, Scrooge is a changed man who remains kind, thoughtful and generous.

Ty notices tears running down Mandy's cheeks. He slips his arm around her and holds her close. She looks up at him, her embarrassment evident, but he loved that she cared. "It's a touching story, isn't it?"

I'm so glad we saw this, Ty. I related in some ways to Scrooge, and—"

"No, Mandy, you're nothing like Scrooge. How can you see a comparison?"

She looked at the ground in front of her. "I focus on me, Ty, and grumble if I don't have things my way. I try to be nice but I have little patience, and I'm ashamed. My mother is an example. I treated her badly, because in my eyes that's what she deserved, but the Bible says to treat others as you want to be treated. It tells us to show compassion and kindness. It's hard to do that when I can't see how those attributes don't benefit me."

Ty drew her closer. "Listen, you're not like that. You do think of others. You were kind and thoughtful to your grandmother, and—"

"Okay, I did treat grandma well, but not everyone. I could go on with the list. Even you, Ty, I've used you in so many ways. You've been doing so much for me, and I rock back and forth with indecision on whether to go back to Chicago or stay here. I know that you'd like me to stay, and you've done everything to make my life wonderful here. I can't continue to do that. I don't want to be Scrooge and think only of myself."

Ty opened his mouth, but before he got a word out, she stopped him again.

"Please don't try to make me feel better. I'll only feel worse, Ty. I need to give you a break. I need to prove that I can show kindness and thoughtfulness to others and not for their praise, but for my acceptance that helping others is something we should do."

"So, what are you saying, Mandy? You don't want to spend time with me and you—"

"No, I'm saying I can't tie you up daily to help me or give me answers or inspire me. I have to learn to do things myself."

"Okay, I'll try to remember not to volunteer then. I'm afraid it might be difficult for me to remember, but I'll do my best."

"I know you will. I've been thinking and I'm trying to make some decisions on my own. When I know what I'm doing and what I'm resolved to do, I'll let you know. You deserve it, Ty. You've been my rescuer for so long, and I want to give you a break. I appreciate everything you've done for me. Everything."

She tiptoed up and her lips rose toward his mouth, but she leaned to the left and brushed his cheek.

His heart sank. The one kiss on his lips had left him longing for another and another. After her new guidelines, he will have to live with the memory. He feared things had changed more than he'd ever expected or wanted.

♥

Mandy paced across the floor like someone waiting for bad news. She'd been fine, but lonely. After her determined talk with Ty, she'd set ground rules that had left her in misery. She'd done it to herself, and she thought it was good. She cared too much for Ty. It took her a long time to realize that life without him seemed no life at all. Their friendship had lasted for years and years from young teens to the present. Now in her early thirties, life had wrapped around Ty except for her years in Chicago, and even then, Ty lay on her mind often. She would go to bed at night reliving memories that made her happy. Most girls had girlfriends. She'd had a few, but they weren't as close or significant as Ty had been. They shared their problems, their dreams, their successes, their failures everything. She had no secrets, and he had none either.

But then the fact left her questioning their relationship. For one, marriage had never tempted her. She'd dated only a few men in Chicago and found no one that could outshine Ty. He was the image she looked for in a serious relationship, and she found no one who could even put a nick in Ty's personality or value. She learned once having a five-carat diamond, made a four-carat stone disappointing.

She'd pondered calling Ty, but her ground rules said no. Not yet.

Needing to do something, an idea struck her and it had meaning. Since the horrible visit with her mother, and she somewhat blamed herself, she still knew nothing. She'd waited too long to get answers from her grandmother who was now in heaven and finding someone who'd known her mother for years wasn't... The thought stumbled. Maybe it was easy.

While her memory reviewed old family friends who might have the answer. With her grandma's funeral in her thoughts, Edith came to mind. She'd been their neighbor for years. Edith knew her mother and grandmother. So perhaps she had her answer. Talk with Edith and learn what she knew.

Her body trembled with the possibility of knowing the answers to her questions for once. She thought about giving up and letting her mother and father have their secrets, but their secrets caused Mandy problems. Marriage frightened her. When she married—if she married—she always wanted to be confident that she and her husband's marriage would cling to the vows they would speak - until death do us part.

Too many people accepted proposals and ended up married without knowing enough about each other and without the familiarity couples marrying should know. Do they have traits or beliefs that the other party can't handler? Do they enjoy similar things in life—going to the movies, camping, hiking, traveling? Do they share a sense of humor? That's one thing that Mandy valued. Laughter is the best medicine. The Bible says it and Mandy agreed. Nothing resolved issues or softened tension as much as laughter. She and Ty often laughed about many things.

She tried to control her memories and her own marriage thoughts, so she emptied her mind. She needed to be open, so she could organize her thoughts when she talked to Edith. And she wanted to do it soon.

♥

A sprinkle of snow lay on the ground when Mandy looked out the window. Though she had watched the calendar and was aware that Christmas was closing in, she had no plans to celebrate the holiday. She'd decided that she and Ty needed to spend time apart. She hadn't anticipated a snowfall, and also hadn't prepared herself for snow without Ty.

They had so much fun in the winter acting like children, throwing snowballs, making a snowman and flinging themselves into fresh snow to make snow angels. Silly, but a treasure in her memory. Since they'd been apart—her fault, her decision—life seemed empty. It reminded her of her grandmother' death and the loneliness she felt when she faced the loss.

Instead of hanging around the house, she knew she needed to do something, and Christmas only three and a half weeks away, provided motivation to get out and shop. She slipped on comfortable shoes and a warm sweater, grasped her coat and headed out the door. Holly didn't have many clothing stores, but it had enough for her to take a look.

The snow had grown heavier so she watched her step as she headed for her car. The ride was short and rock salt had been spread on the highway so for now driving was safe. She went to the main shopping area and found a parking spot. Though she didn't need anything for herself, she still wanted to give Ty a Christmas gift even though she and Ty had taken a break.

The first store she spotted was Creative Fashion. Women's clothes. She shrugged and headed inside. A turquoise and pistachio blouse caught her eye. The colors were swirled into a contemporary pattern. She had slacks and a skirt that could be worn with the blouse.

Maybe it wasn't so bad to buy herself a Christmas present. She grinned at her attempt to play innocent with herself.

Playing it safe, she stepped outside, fearing she'd find another top that she liked. Her goal was a gift for Ty. She'd stood a moment watching the flakes settle on her jacket sleeve and trying to recall where she could find a men's store.

"Amanda Cahill. It's been years."

Mandy spun around and studied the handsome face of someone who apparently knew her.

He grinned. "It's been many years so it's okay you

can't remember." He approached her and stood surveying her from head to toe. "You're still gorgeous. Maybe even more than in high school."

High school. At least she had half a chance to recall who he was. "Nice to see you, too."

He stuck out his hand. "Allen Green. We took an art class together and a math class. Geometry, if I remember correctly. And I asked you to the Junior prom, but you already had a date."

"Allen Green. I'm so sorry I didn't recognize you. You're as handsome as ever, but my memory short-circuited, I believe."

He grinned. "So, where have you been?"

"Chicago. But my grandmother died so I came back for her funeral and learned that I inherited everything she had."

"Wow, that must have been a shock. I'm sorry about your grandmother."

"Thanks. She is a huge loss. I don't know if you remember, but I lived with her for a while. My parents split and my mother left town, so I only had my dad, and then he died a few years after my mother left, so I was an orphan of sorts."

"Tough times for you." He looked at his watch. "Listen, it's lunch time. Are you in a hurry? I'd love to talk a while."

Mandy studied him a moment and decided he wasn't approaching her for anything more than conversation. "Sure. That would be nice, Al." She studied his expression. "That is what we called you right?"

"Sure is. It sounds more natural to me than Allen."

"Okay, then. Where are we going?"

"How about River Rock Grill? Great burgers and they have fries plus French-fried onion sticks."

"I love those. It sounds great."

She pointed out her car, but he suggested they walk. They reminisced about high school parties and dances. Fun things they recalled and laughed at the crazy things they had done. When they were seated in the grill and had placed their order, Al leaned back and glanced at her hands. "Not married?"

"No, I spent a long time working in Chicago, and I didn't find it a great place to fall in love."

"Really?" Al arched a brow. "That's hard to believe. You've always been good-looking, and I'm surprised someone didn't catch your interest."

"Oh, it was me. I wasn't interested in getting involved. I looked forward to being independent for a while and enjoying life. Marriage didn't interest me, and I'm still a bit leery, although I have a wonderful friend that if I were interested, he would be the one."

Al's face lit up. "Don't tell me. I just remembered. Tyler Evans. The two of you seemed glued together, but it always seemed more like friends than anything else."

She nodded. "That was it, and we've been great friends all this time. I think we've both had parent issues to make us wonder about successful marriages, and neither of us have been able to move away from the bad examples."

"That's too bad, Amanda. You're missing out on something special."

"I don't see a ring on your finger, or do you take it off when you meet a new woman?"

He gave her a crooked smile. "That's somewhat an

insult, but I'll assume you're kidding. No, I'm not a rover. I was engaged, and she walked away."

"You're kidding?"

"Nope. That put a bad taste in my mouth, and I haven't trusted much of anything sense then."

"Sorry. I really am."

"I can believe that." As the words left him, the waitress arrived with their burgers and fries.

They silenced, and Mandy bit into her burger. She'd forgotten how good they were, especially the one she'd ordered.

Al took a large bite, and when they'd both finished the burgers, they talked a little and nibbled on the fries until Mandy noticed the time. "I better get moving. I have a neighbor I need to talk with and I don't want to go over there too late."

"I'm really glad I ran into you, Amanda."

She thought about telling him to call her Mandy, but it didn't seem worth it. "Good to see you too, Al."

He turned sideways and tilted his head toward the far side of the grill. "Isn't that Tyler Evans over there."

"Tyler?" Her heart skipped as she eased around for a quick look and then turned back. "Yes, it is." She sensed she should say more or go over and say hello, but it didn't fit the distance she wanted to have for a while. She had to sort out her feelings, but right now her own feeling was guilt.

She opened her bag and pulled out her wallet.

"Hey, this one's on me, Amanda."

"Al, no. I—"

"It's on me. I can afford a burger and fries. Please I've enjoyed seeing you and talking about old times. Please let me do this."

She didn't want to make a fool of herself, so she nodded, and when she tried to stand her legs felt weak. If Ty saw her with Al, he would think she tossed him out for another man. She couldn't bear thinking that she might have hurt him or confused him. She cared too much.

Her pulse did a dance that rattled her, and what else rattled her was if she cared so much why had she asked for time apart? It made no sense."

♥

Three more days passed without talking to Ty, and her nerves were raw, and her heart ached. She missed him more than she'd expected, yet she should have known, and now fearing that he saw her in the grill with Al would really confuse the situation.

She tried to occupy her thoughts with questions she had for Edith, and today she'd decided to call Edith and see if she had time to talk. Her pulse galloped when Edith said she had plenty of time to talk, and the one surprise was she didn't ask what Mandy wanted to talk about.

Mandy gathered her questions from the table and tucked them in her pocket. But as she stepped away, she faltered. Drawing in a breath, she asked herself if asking Edith had been a wise idea. That would put Edith in a bad situation, and she hated to do that. Still she wanted answers. Needed answers if she were ever going to become a wife and hopefully a mother.

She sent up a quick prayer that her decision would not hurt anyone and braced herself as she stepped outside. Edith lived right next door so the walk took seconds, and when she stepped onto the porch, Edith opened the door as if she'd been waiting. "Come in, Mandy. It's good to see you."

"Thanks, and another thanks for being willing to talk. I've been a bit lonely lately and that's the kind of time that causes me to think too much, and I begin digging up questions. So, here I am."

"First, have a seat and then would you like a pop or a cup of tea?"

Mandy thought a moment "Pop is fine."

Edith headed for the kitchen and returned with a glass of something pale yellow and frizzy. "I remembered you like ginger ale. Is that right?"

"Love it." Mandy smiled. "And I'm guessing it's Vernors."

"You guessed right. I'm guessing you probably couldn't always get that in Chicago."

"You're right about that too." They both chuckled as Edith settled in a nearby easy chair. "You aroused my curiosity, Mandy."

"I did?" She studied Edith's expression. "In what way?"

"Telling me you're lonely. Where's Ty?"

"That's a different story, but I guess the stories are connected in a way. I suppose I can answer that first before the main story." Mandy swallowed, fearing she would break down and sob if she didn't get a grip on herself.

"I made a rash decision, Edith, and I think I'm doing Ty a disservice. We care about each other, but I don't think I'll ever marry, and it isn't fair to him."

"Never marry? Mandy, why? You're a wonderful person, and marriage is a kind of fulfillment if you want to be a parent." Edith looked down and shook her head.

"I don't understand?"

Mandy took a sip of the pop and thought a moment. "Let me start here. First, if I make you uncomfortable, Edith, please tell me."

"I'm not usually uncomfortable so go ahead."

Mandy gathered her thoughts and began with what she'd been struggling with. "I want to understand my parents' miserable marriage. Their relationship couldn't fool anyone. They barely talked, and I never understood why they married and why they stuck it out when they lived as two strangers."

Edith looked away for a moment, leaving Mandy confused. She'd never thought Edith would not want to give her some explanation. "Edith, I'm sorry. I don't want to—"

"Listen, don't be sorry. I'm not certain why you feel that someone's bad marriage can influence you. You're you, and your relationship with a man who becomes your husband will be based on your ability to love and communicate. My guess is that you would never get involved with someone who didn't communicate well with you or someone you didn't love."

"Right, but people make mistakes." Ty's image filled her thoughts, but she didn't want to stop now. "I've often heard people who say their marriage ended due to lack of communication."

"But you're too wise to do that, Mandy. You are a communicator. You're talking with me and expressing yourself well. You've been friends—devoted friends with Ty all these years, and I know you two communicate. I've seen it happening, and it's good."

A ragged breath fluttered from Mandy's lungs. "But I have my parent's genes, and I can't help but be confused and not understand. Edith, I promise with all my heart that if you tell me about my parents' marriage, I will never say a word to my mom. It's for me to understand so I can make sure I'm not looking at life and love with their eyes. Does that make sense?"

"Oh, Mandy, it does, and I do understand. I can comprehend why you're concerned, so let me tell you what I know."

"Thank you, Edith. Thank you so much. I really think that if I understand, I won't see it as a monster hiding somewhere waiting to pounce on my life."

Edith's eyes widened. "You've felt that way?"

Mandy nodded. "I have, yes."

"Don't. You have no need. If you marry, you'll marry for love and companionship. You'll be dear friends, just as you and Ty have had an amazing relationship all these years."

Ty, again, his face filled her mind. Handsome, but that wasn't the best. He cared about her, and it was obvious. He had every attribute that she'd ever wanted in a husband. He was the dearest, sweetest person in her life, and yet they called it a friendship. She'd questioned that title lately. Life wouldn't be the same without Ty.

"Are you ready, Mandy?"

She drew in a lengthy breath. "Ready as I'll ever be. It's been on my mind for too long."

"Okay. I'm sure there are things you don't know about your parents. Their relationship was nothing like yours and Ty's. You became dear friends and have spent much of your life together in that way. But now, I sense that friendship has grown into something deeper and more precious."

A chill rolled down Mandy's spine. Deeper and precious. Edith was right.

"I want you to stop me if you don't want to hear it all, Mandy. It's not a pretty story."

"I knew it couldn't be, Edith. My parents were like strangers living together so nothing will surprise me, but maybe I'll better understand how it all happened."

Edith nodded, and then eyed her for a moment before she began. "Here we go." She wet her lips. "Your dad apparently had been casual friends with your mother. I'm not sure how they met, but your mother got pregnant, and your father found out. He had not slept with your mother, but he felt sorry for her being unmarried and now expecting some man's child, a man who walked away from your mother."

"That sounds like my dad."

"Having married her, your dad began to fall in love with her, but your mother's love wasn't reciprocated.

"That sounds like my mother."

"But she ended up losing the baby, and though your mother seemed to find it easy to walk away, this time she didn't. She made an effort to be a wife to your dad, and that's when she conceived you, and she remained married to your dad.

"If she did that, then what happened? She married again right after my dad died. She must have had someone lined up."

"It wasn't quite like that, Mandy. Apparently, the man who walked away when she was pregnant regretted his action, and he returned to ask her back into his life, but your mother didn't leave. She remained faithful to your dad until he died. Then she was free to return to the man she'd loved so long. So, it appeared that she ran off with a stranger after your dad died, but that isn't what happened."

Mandy's chest ached as she relived those horrible feelings she'd experienced for what she thought had been her mother's actions. Now she understood and wished she'd known the truth before.

"Edith, I can't thank you enough for letting me know the truth. I forgive my mother for what I had misconstrued, and I hope she can forgive me for my horrible attitude.

"I'm sure she will, Mandy, and now I hope that you can look at marriage with a clearer vision and not mess up your future with a wonderful man, because of what you thought. Life is complicated and sometimes we have to step back and search for the truth. Remember the saying from the Bible, 'The truth can set you free.' It can, and I hope you'll let it."

"I can't thank you enough for explaining this to me, Edith, I had everything wrong."

"But you had reason to be confused. You didn't have the facts. You do now."

"And I am grateful. I hope I've learned a lesson not to read into things when I don't know the details."

"That's a good thing to remember, Mandy."

Mandy rose and moved closer to Edith. She opened her arms and gave Edith a hug. "I can't thank you enough."

"You already did. I hope the next time you see your mother, you can smooth over some of the bad feelings. I really believe that both of you will be happier."

"I know I will, Edith. I'm happier now knowing what you told me. It makes sense, and again, it's knowing the truth."

She hugged Edith again and said goodbye. Her next important job was to talk with Ty, ask for forgiveness and tell him how much he means to her. Then, she would open her arms and kiss him the way she'd longed to do.

♥

On the way home snowflakes drifted down, clinging to the windshield. Mandy spotted the grill and decided to stop for lunch. Though she didn't feel hungry, her stomach thought it was. It's grumbling embarrassed her when others heard it. When she walked in, she paused to look for an empty table. Instead of finding a table, she spotted Ty sitting with Lauren at a table almost hidden in a corner.

Her chest tightened, nearly crushing her lungs. She closed her eyes willing away what she had seen. Lauren's face glowed as she leaned toward Ty as if sharing a secret. Bitter and confused, Mandy longed to march up to the table and face them, but it would be useless. Ty had every right to have lunch with whomever he chose. She was the one who told him they needed a break.

A waitress who noticed her standing in the middle of the floor, pointed to an empty table across the room. Her appetite vanished, and a need to get out of the grill without being seen became her priority. Feeling foolish, she told the waitress she changed her mind. The waitress apologized, as if she'd done something wrong, and Mandy felt ridiculous. She wanted to explain, but what could she say that wouldn't make her even more ludicrous.

When a patron beckoned to the waitress, Mandy

grasped the chance to leave before Ty saw her. Outside, she faltered, seeing snow piling against the curb and on her windshield. As the damp air chilled her bones, she had little choice. If she wanted to drive, she had to clear the windows. She dug in the backseat for her scrapper and began pushing the snow off the glass. She hadn't worn gloves and her feet felt wet.

Tears flooded her eyes, but she knew the emotion had little to do with the cold snow. What pained her was having told Ty they needed a break, and he'd followed her request, a request she'd made to feel in charge and not admit she'd made a dire mistake.

Looking through blurred eyes, she took another swipe at the car's roof, knowing the snow would slide back down on the windows if she didn't.

"Can I help you, Mandy?"

She froze in place, certain that the voice was Ty's. Having to face Lauren dragged her tears down her cheeks.

Ty touched her arm. "Let me help you. You're freezing." He reached across her and pulled the scraper from her hand. "Why don't you get in the car and start it. You need to warm up before you get yourself sick.

Instead of fighting his offer, she looked at his beautiful face and gave a faint nod. "Thank you, Ty. I had no idea the snow would fall so fast." She looked around, not seeing Lauren. "Where's your fri...Lauren?"

"She left when she saw the snow." He opened her driver's door. "Now get in and start the car."

His insistence made sense. She'd begun to shiver so bad that her teeth clattered together. Through the window, she watched him drag the snow off the car and clean the windows. Her heart sang, so happy to see him, and though she didn't understand why Lauren had her own car, she didn't care. Lauren was gone.

When Ty cleared the snow the best he could, new snow continued to fall. He knocked on her window, and she rolled it down. "Ty, do you need a ride?"

"No, my car is here. I didn't ride with Lauren. I was here, and she just happened to come in so she sat with me."

Her concern lightened, hearing his explanation. "I'm so glad you're here, Ty. I've been wanting to—"

"I'm glad too, since I may have saved you from getting pneumonia." He grinned.

"No that's not it. I've been wanting to talk with you, and here you are."

"I've missed you, Mandy. We've been friends for too many years to take a vacation from each other and I'm not sure why you wanted to do that."

She wasn't sure either, but she needed an explanation. "I've been mixed up, Ty, and confused." An icy chill ran down her back.

He rested his arm on the window's edge. "Why are we doing this? You're freezing and so am I. Let's go somewhere if you really want to talk, and I believe you do."

"You're right. So, is it my house? Your house? I've never been inside your house, Ty. Did you know that? You didn't have your own home when I lived in Holly."

Ty's eyes widened. "Really. I guess that's true. How about your house? I've never been one to invite women to my house, but then you're not just any woman."

His comment took a moment to interpret, but once she did, she grinned. "I'm glad to hear that, but what am I if I'm not just any woman?"

"Let's talk about that later when we're not freezing."

Mandy gave him a playful poke. "Okay, but I know the real reason why. You probably haven't cleaned in days."

"Wrong, but I have my reasons." He lowered his arm and pointed behind her. "Since I have my car, I'll follow you to your house. It's getting slippery, but I'll be right there if something happens."

"Can I drive you to your car?"

"I just pointed it out. It's two cars behind you. Pull out and I'll follow." He brushed new flakes from the window edge. "And be careful."

"I always am." But she figured Ty knew better.

Ty headed toward his car and she backed out. When her wheels slipped, her heart rose to her throat. She'd just missed clipping the car behind her. She hoped Ty hadn't noticed.

When she eased into the street, Ty's car appeared in her rearview mirror. She slowed and prayed that she and Ty got home safely. She didn't remember such a heavy snowfall that came on so fast.

Her heart lurched when she saw her street. She slowed even more to make the turn. She'd noticed cars sliding even though they were going slow. Once in the driveway, she rolled to the garage, opened the door and parked inside. Before she turned off the motor, Ty had pulled up close to the backdoor.

She slipped out of the seat and met Ty outside. He clutched her arm against his as he guided her to the back door. She pulled the key from her purse and unlocked it. "You were right, Ty, I've never experienced such slippery snow. Not even in Chicago?"

"I'm guessing Chicago has a system to get salt on the road for self-defense before the snow falls. Big cities have so much traffic, they have no choice."

"That makes sense. I didn't think of that." Once again, Ty had the answers to her questions even before she asks him. "You're a smart man, Mr. Evans."

"Why so formal?" He wiped his shoes off on the matt.

"I don't invite men to my house either, but then you're not just any man."

He gave her one of those you-caught-me looks. "Okay, I fell for it."

Mandy pushed open the door and waved Ty inside. She followed, nervous, but happy that they had time to talk, and yet, some of the things she wanted to talk about would take courage. "Sit anywhere you want, Ty, and would you like something hot to drink. I can make coffee or tea or how about some hot chocolate."

"Do you have to ask?" Ty winked.

"Okay, hot chocolate it is." She headed for the cabinet where she recalled putting the cocoa mix. She found it without a problem, read the recipe and followed it. Five minutes later, she carried two mugs into the living room and gave one to Ty. "I'll confess, this isn't totally homemade, but it's still good and I added some mini-marshmallows."

She took the spoon and stirred the now white liquid in the mug. Before she tasted it, Ty indicated he liked it by his "Mmm" sound.

"Glad you like it."

Ty eyed her. "Was I that obvious?"

Mandy mimicked his interjection. "What do you think?"

They laughed together, and the happy sound put Mandy at ease. "That's one thing I love about us. We laugh together, we have fun together, and when we share something serious, we support each other."

"So…you love that about us."

"I do. I don't have anyone in my life like you, Ty. That's why I feel lost without you."

"Really?" He studied her face and put her on edge.

"I'm not making it up. I'm being honest."

"I know. I feel the same. These past weeks that you suggested a 'vacation' from each other was no vacation. It was a horror movie. I kept looking over my shoulder, trying to make sense out of it and us."

Mandy's heart picked up pace and the beats struck her chest. "Ty, I do want to talk about this too, but I hope it's okay that I change the subject for a moment since I've learned something important since I saw you last, and I can't tell the story to just anyone. As always, it's something I want to tell you."

Concern marred his face. "Did I do something wrong?"

"You? No. You don't know how to do something wrong, Ty. I talked to Edith. You know her."

"Yes, she was your grandmother's neighbor."

"Right and she knew not only my grandma, but also my parents. And she told me about their life together. I could never understand why they married and why they stayed together as long as they did. Now, I know."

"Mandy, I'm happy for you. I know that troubled you since I've met you. I never knew exactly why, but—"

"Ty, the reason why is I have their genes, and I observed their life together like two strangers with nothing in common and nothing that showed love. I grew up thinking that must be what marriage is."

"You're kidding, right?"

"No. That was the role model I observed for years until my mother left and then my dad died. My grandmother was the only stable person in my life, except you."

"Thank you, Mandy, but my life wasn't perfect either. My parents have always been supportive, but they're not ones to gush. I never realized that I missed hearing words like love, good-looking, talented or intelligent. I questioned myself so often. I couldn't comprehend why you were my friend, and yet you were a faithful, kind and caring friend who I could trust. I used to compare myself to other people I knew, people in school that you knew. In fact, when I spotted you with Al Green, I felt lost."

"Lost? Why would you feel that way and about Al?"

"Al is handsome, very handsome. I often heard girls talk about his good looks and hoping he would ask them out. Some of these girls were ones I asked to a school dance or event, but I often got a 'thanks anyway' since they were going out with Al or some other good-looking guy. I'm not handsome, Mandy. I figured you were such a good friend you didn't care that I wasn't good-looking. You were still a good friend."

Mandy sank back against the chair cushion, trying to deal with what Ty had admitted. "What gave you an idea that you aren't good-looking,

Ty? And are good looks more important than attributes? To me, you are kind, thoughtful, caring, strong, funny, generous. I could go on and on, and to me you are handsome. You have amazing hair, black with a shine like the sun, a wonderful smile, and you know I love your blue eyes."

"You've never told me this me before."

Mandy's jaw dropped as she leaned forward. "Why would I? I thought you knew how much I thought of you. Why would I be your best friend if I didn't see those attributes, and yes, I think you're great looking. I'd say you're handsome."

Ty, looked startled, his jaw limp, his eyes shifting like a search light. "I...I'm speechless."

"You?' Mandy stared at him like a statue. "When have you been speechless, Ty?"

"Right now." He shook his head. "I had lots of other things to say, but I think I need to digest this part of our conversation before I add anything else. I might scare you away."

"Never. Never. You're too much a part of my life."

He rose from the couch and shifted closer to her. "Why not tell me about your parents? I'd love to hear what you learned. I know that something you've wanted to understand for years."

"It was, but now I know and even better I understand. I'd like to tell you too, so you can comprehend why it's been such a hush-hush story."

Mandy's face said a lot, and Ty sensed that listening to the story would help her relax and weigh what it all means. They could evaluate the situation together, as they did so often. He leaned back and heard the difficult story that Mandy had longed to understand most of her life.

When she finished, Ty rose from the couch and drew her into his arms. "Your situation is much more difficult than anything I had to live with, Mandy. No wonder you needed someone who cared enough about you and someone that you were confident with to talk about your concerns."

"Ty, I wouldn't tell anyone else what I told you today, but I am at ease knowing that you know and knowing that it's between us. I never fear that you'd share it with others, and I know I can trust you, Ty. I assured Edith that I would never tell my parents' story to anyone, but I've already broken that guarantee, and yet I don't worry because I know you are a friend whose relationship with me is impossible for most people to understand."

"Sometimes I don't understand it either, but I'd be lost without you, Mandy."

"Same with me, Ty. In fact, let's take a step back to the conversation we started before my parents' story. I think I'm ready."

His quizzical look gave her a jolt, but when he nodded, she knew he understood. "So, let's go back to us. After I realized I don't have to fear having some of my parents' genes. I'm no longer fearful of marriage. I want to marry a man whom I know, trust and love, a person who will laugh with me, and have the answers before I ask the question."

"Good luck on that list of attributes, my dear. Those people are hard to find."

She dug out her courage and hung on. "I don't have to find him, Ty. I know him already."

"Al Green." Ty's jaw dropped as his head jerked

backward and his eyes widened. "I hadn't really thought—"

"Ty." She reached out and grasped his arm. "Think, Ty. I've never had any feelings for Al, other than we went to school together. I don't see him, unless we bump into each other as we did the other day. That was the first time I'd seen him in years."

"That's why I'm surprised, Mandy."

"Ty, think logically. What man do I spend more time with than anyone else?"

He sat a moment as if confused. "Me. That's the only person I can think of."

"Good, because that's correct. It's you that I spend my time with. It's you that has all those wonderful attributes. It's you that I would marry."

Ty's eyes sparkled like a Christmas tree. "Marry? I never considered marriage, because you always said you would never marry."

"That was before I heard my mother and father's story. Now I know I'm safe from following in their footsteps."

"Then you can give thought to marriage. What about having children?"

"I'm confident now that I have good genes, I would love to have children. So, yes, I want to have children."

"So do I, and I didn't give thought to marriage, because the only woman I wanted to marry said she would never marry."

"Who said something that fina..?"

"You did, Mandy. You said it and it broke my heart. You're the only woman that I have ever loved."

"Ty, we're friends. Best friends. This has weighed on my mind since I seriously looked into my heart. Can we really—?"

"What's the option? I could walk away and try to mend my heart and find someone who loves me enough to—"

"No, Ty. This conversation doesn't make sense."

"You're right. It makes no sense at all. I've had too much on my mind, learning all this about my parents, and I don't think you're ready to think through things. Let's hold on. The days are short now with winter on our backs. Christmas is here in a few weeks, and we have things do to."

"Like what?" Ty studied her face but gave up. She looked confused, and he was right. The conversation would go nowhere. At least no where he wanted to go." Ty dragged in a breath. "Let's think about Christmas and give ourselves a break. We've both been trying to figure out too many things. How about enjoying the holiday and then sorting through our thoughts?"

"I'm not a fan of that plan, Ty, but I'll try. By the way, I found Christmas ornaments in my grandmother's attic. Will you help me decorate the tree?"

"I can. Do you have a tree?"

Mandy shifted her eyes. "Grandma had a little tabletop tree. I want a real Christmas tree."

Ty pressed his lips together, trying to stop his response, but he failed. "Can you manipulate a large tree into your car and then into the house?"

"No, but I have a very good friend who will help me."

He looked heavenward. "I think I know him. Okay, when?"

"It's getting dark now and it's still snowing. How about tomorrow?"

"I do have to spend some time at the store, but I'll work out something. And I suppose you need help stringing the lights and decorating too."

Mandy drew closer to him, her eyes seeming to be on his mouth. "I have that friend I mentioned."

"I figured." His pulse skipped, seeing her search his face. Before he could move, Mandy's mouth touched his, her lips soft and warm pressing against his, and his knees began to melt. But instead of stopping her, he drew her closer, parting his lips and moving them in small circles until she moaned. The joy that filled him was nothing that he had experienced before.

Mandy eased back with a faint gasp. "I'll decorate the tree myself, Ty, if you kiss me that way again.

He loved the idea, but he also loved her, and he wanted to be part of their first Christmas together filled with possibilities. "Let's buy the tree tomorrow. It should be in the stand for a day or so before decorating. How's that sound?

"Excellent. I'll bring down the Christmas boxes I found and see if the lights work and what else is there." She remained close reliving his kiss.

"Good idea." But he had another idea of his own. Ty bent closer and captured her lips again. Her kisses had become his obsession.

Chapter 9

Mandy carried one the boxes down from the attic, but coming down a ladder with the box sent goose flesh down her back. She'd already been cumbersome on a ladder and had been warned by Ty, so she pulled the boxes to the edge and waited for him to carry them down.

She was in no rush since they still had to pick out a tree…maybe two trees. Ty never talked about having his own home, and every time he headed that way, she began to think he lived with his parents. The feeling troubled her. Most men would never admit to living with their parents, so the whole idea confused her, and the idea that she had never asked him, concerned her even more.

A car door closing alerted her that Ty had arrived, and with the odd thoughts bouncing through her head troubled her. If he didn't tell her he lived with his parents, she would out and out ask. She waited, but when he didn't come to the door, she gave in and opened it, ready to ask if something was wrong.

Instead, Ty stepped onto the porch, dragging a large fir tree. "Why didn't you ask me to help you, Ty?" She studied his face, noting and waiting for a response. He shrugged and moved forward as if determined to get the tree into the house.

She stood blocking the door and didn't budge.

Ty's forehead wrinkled as he stared at her. "What's up with you? I don't want you trying to help with the tree. You could slip and fall, Mandy. It's very slippery." As the words left his mouth, his feet did exactly that, and landed on top of the tree, back on the sidewalk.

Mandy bounded down the steps, her own feet sliding as she landed beside Ty, on top of the tree. When they looked at each other, they burst into laughter.

Ty tried to pull his feet out of the limbs without tromping on the tree. "Great job. Do I get a medal?" He pulled one foot to the sidewalk and didn't move while Mandy covered her mouth trying to hide her laughter, but she failed.

She gave up and let her giggles bubble from her chest. "Sorry, but we must look like clowns."

Ty shook his head. "Never. No red nose."

She gave him a teasing swat, nearly losing her footing again. "I think we're more dangerous than funny. Let's get this tree inside before we break a leg or an arm."

"Wise choice." He stepped away from the limbs as best he could and helped her to move down to the top of the tree. "If you can lift the top limb, I'll carry the bottom."

She dug her hand into the branches and lifted her end of the shapely fir while he hoisted the bottom. Walking with measured steps, he backed through the doorway and she followed. "Ty, I'll get the tree stand and hopefully, we can get it to stand straight."

"Hopefully." Ty gave her a wink. "Hold it as straight as you can while I get the legs in place and then I'll tighten the eyebolts."

She knelt on the floor struggling to keep the tree straight as he tightened it. "Let the tree go, Mandy and I'll back up and see if it's really straight." He stepped back and applauded. "Okay, we did it."

She joined him admiring the full limbs that were shaped perfectly. "It's a beautiful tree, Ty. Did you buy one for yourself?"

He lifted his brows as if her question were ridiculous and startling.

"I'll buy one later. I have a small tabletop tree."

"And that's all?" His lack of Christmas spirit dragged air from her lungs. "You surprise me, Ty. I thought I knew you, but maybe I don't."

"Mandy, you're making a big deal out of this."

She couldn't respond. She and Ty spent much of their time laughing and teasing each other, but not today. His reaction disappointed her, and she didn't understand.

♥

Ty stood staring into space and unable to understand why having a tabletop tree had become so dramatic. It wasn't like Mandy to react that way.

Sure, he could stand there and stumble over a response, but that wasn't his plan, and trying to explain would ruin it. His response would surprise her, but not in the way he wanted to explain. Astound her is what he wanted.

Her reaction left him both confused and concerned and trying to put it in plain words would ruin everything.

"We can't do anything today, Mandy. The tree needs to stand for a day at least, so I'm going to take care of some things I need to do, and I'll talk with you tomorrow." He didn't wait for a response, but backed up a few steps and then spun around and hurried to the door, hating what had happened but having no other way to fix it.

During his drive home, an idea burst into his mind. He could not only fix his problem, but he prayed his action would both surprise her and fill her with happiness. At least he hoped that could happen.

Before he reached home, he turned off where he knew he would find a Christmas tree lot. Wanting to let Mandy know how much he loved her, he longed to kick himself for his unneeded comment about having only a table tree. Yes, he had one, but it was a gift from his parents when he first moved into an apartment. It meant something to him.

Ty parked and headed down the first row of trees. He knew what he liked, a tall tree that would fit in his living room with the cathedral ceilings. He wandered up and down the rows and finally spotted what he'd wanted. A perfect balsam fir with a dark green color, heavy density foliage and short needles. Its solid branches could hold even large ornaments. His heart skipped, knowing that Mandy would love the tree.

The tree lot proprietor helped him tie the tree to the roof of his car, and he headed home, hoping he could get it into the house without help. He questioned the possibility but had no choice.

When he pulled into his driveway, his neighbor had stepped out of his home and paused. "Hey, Ty. Now that's what I call a tree. Can I help you?"

A huge smile curved Ty's lips as he approached his neighbor. "Sam, you are the answer to my prayers. I bought the tree without thinking it through. I wanted to surprise my lady friend. I know you haven't met her since I've never brought her here."

Sam's grin faded to a frown. "You are kidding."

"No, she and I have been best friends for years,

and—"

"She's never been here? Sam's eyes widened. "You're not kidding when you say you want to surprise her."

"I have my reasons. Our best friend status, after all these years, has changed. Really changed.

"Ty, I hope this is a good change."

He eyed Sam, a moment. "I'm in love with her, and I am fairly confident that she feels the same."

"Man, you do take changes. You are fairly confident? I hope you're correct."

Sam's commen, shook that fairly confident faith and made him pause. "Okay, Sam, I'm praying I'm right."

"I'll join you in that prayer, Ty. So how about I help you get the tree inside. Are you going to have her help decorate or—"

"I was tossing the idea around. She can help or I could really surprise her with it decorated when she first sees it."

Sam patted his shoulder. "I say decorate it. That's a huge job."

"You're right. It could take me days."

"Here's an idea. If I ask my wife and even my two teens if they would help, I'm guessing they will. The boys are always talking about your huge tree and want one too. We don't have cathedral ceilings, and Jan would help, I'm sure."

"Sam, you could be a lifesaver. Check with your wife and those boys and let me know. I could probably use help getting it into the stand."

"I'll ask now, and let you know."

Ty couldn't believe that he'd been so stupid to buy

a tree that he couldn't handle on his own, but the situation with Mandy had messed up his commonsense. He hurried inside and ran down to the basement pulling up the large boxes full of ornaments and tree lights. Before he made it up the stairs, Sam called to him saying they were on their way."

His determination that the tree sit for a day or two before decorating it fell by the wayside. To accept help when you can get it was more important.

Sam, his wife Jan and his twin sons, Michael and Mitchell bound into the house with more enthusiasm than Ty had expected.

"Thanks so much friends. I didn't think things through, and I would be in a mess without your wonderful volunteering."

Sam gave Ty a pat on the back. "That's what friends are for Ty."

While he and Sam set up the tree, Jan checked the tree lights while the boys searched for bulbs that needed replacing. Once the tree stood straight and just missing the ceiling, the twins took turns climbing the ladder to string the lights, while the other one held the ladder for safety.

Once the lights filled the limbs, Sam and Ty hung the Christmas balls near the top while the twins and Jan worked below. With everyone's help and enthusiasm, Ty's head spun. He'd questioned his tall tree choice, but the job was nearly done.

He took a break and called a popular pizzeria. It was getting late and he was grateful for the help. He ordered a large antipasti salad and two large pizzas. When the food arrived, the group had nearly finished decorating. The tree looked great and he couldn't thank them enough.

Sam ate his fourth piece if pizza, which he admitted, and even his boys laughed. More grateful than he could explain, he thanked them again. The pleasure of having great neighbors had touched Ty. He'd always tried to be friendly and nice to people, but Sam, Jan and the boys did more than anyone would expect. They even gathered the boxes and asked where he wanted them to go. He had them put in one of the guest rooms, and when they left, he caved into his recliner and reviewed how much they had accomplished. Tomorrow he would see Mandy and help decorate her tree before he surprised her not only with a tree, but a house he'd kept a secret until a special day. Since Christmas seemed a good time, his surprise would be soon.

♥

The next morning, Mandy, did her best to string lights on the tree. She used the step stool and feared falling, since Ty was always worried about that, although she finished the lights and patted herself on the back. What did Ty know?

Her sarcastic thought caught her off guard. Making snide comments about Ty turned her stomach. She and Ty had been lifelong friends and treating him in any other way upset her, even though that was what she'd just done.

"Stop it, Amanda." She spoke aloud, using her formal name rather than the one that friends used. Today she no longer saw herself as a friend, and she wanted to understand if she and Ty had distance themselves or if she was confused. What had changed their relationship didn't set well in her mind. How could two people who'd been best friends for years decide to end the relationship.

A shiver ran down her spine as she struggled to make sense out of what had happened. He'd kissed her and she'd kissed him back, and for the first time, she sensed that maybe a deeper relationship wasn't meant to be. The thought brought tears to her eyes, and she hurried into the bathroom to grab a tissue.

As she wandered back into the living room, a knock sounded at the door, and she froze. Facing Ty now dug at her heart. What could she say, or didn't he realize what had happened when they were together the day before? It had all been too much too fast, and it left her totally confused.

She heard the knock again so it couldn't be Ty. He would have opened the door and called her name. Mandy and not Amanda. Instead of guessing, she headed for the door. When she opened it, Ty stared at her. "Are you alright?"

"I don't know. I…"

"You're upset with me, and I'm sorry, Mandy. I can't explain it either. I've asked myself over and over while I tried to guess if we've lost our friendship or ruined it with the changing our relationship to something different. Were the kisses—?

"I loved your kisses, Ty. I agree it was somewhat of a surprise, but I had the feeling, one day it would happen. My feelings grew stronger than they had been, and I'm not a fool. In fact, when I saw you that day with Lauren, I'll admit that I became very jealous."

Ty moved closer and clasped her hand. "And when I saw you with Allen Green, I felt the same way."

She eyed him, asking herself if it were true. "I'm certain that our reasons to feel jealous meant something to both of us. Jealousy has to do with fearing a rival, but I'm thinking that it also shows our lack of confidence in the relationship. Do you feel that way?"

"Mandy, I think jealousy is one of those things that makes a person think that they don't deserve the relationship or it's too good to be true."

"Or maybe we fear that we're doing something that God doesn't approve."

"That's hard for me to accept, Mandy. Why would God let our friendship go on for years if He didn't approve? I never felt sinful because I cared about you as much as I have."

"You're right, Ty. Our relationship has been amazing, and I can't believe either, that it's wrong."

Then, my dearest friend, let's accept who we are and what we feel and believe. "You are more important to me, Mandy, than many things in my life. I believe that our relationship is changing. It's deeper and more beautiful than—"

She pressed her index finger on his lips and drew closer while her heart pounded. She tiptoed to kiss him, but this kiss was different. Her heart leaped as her lips sought his, lingering in pleasure as he took her breath away.

Ty curved his arm around her and held her close. "I have an idea, Mandy. Let's decorate your tree, and then I want to take you somewhere. I think you'll like it."

She studied him a moment, her mouth easing open as if to ask a question, and then she stopped. "Surprise me, Ty."

He knew he would, and he relaxed sensing that this

time, she really wanted to be surprised.

♥

While Ty circled Mandy's tree with strings of lights, she selected red and green beads and wove them through the branches. They both selected ornaments—colorful balls and wreaths, sparkling angels and stars, the nativity, and shepherd's crooks. Mandy located a golden harp and a wooden drum. The limbs became filled with symbols of Christmas.

"I think we're done, Ty. I could squeeze some more on the branches, but I think it looks pretty."

"So do I, Mandy. What do you say? Ready to go?"

"I am, especially since I'm curious."

He grinned and gave her a wink. "I like you that way."

"Not fair, Ty."

He gave her a sideways look, trying to draw out her curiosity. "Sure it's fair, Mandy. Anything's fair that's truthful."

She gave him a poke. "I'm not going to let you win. I'll tell you if it's fair later."

He didn't respond, knowing he would tempt her to challenge him about being fair.

He hooked her arm in his and guided her down the porch steps, wanting to make sure that she didn't slip. The snow had turned into ice, and not only was driving difficult but walking was as bad.

Instead of pulling into his driveway, he'd contacted Sam, asking to use his driveway. Since it was wide, Sam could still pull in. When he parked at Sam's, Mandy didn't take her eyes off his house next to Sam's. "Now that's a house." She pointed to his home.

"It is a good size. You'd think Sam had tons of children but he doesn't."

Though his plan helped with his surprise, he did feel unfair now that he'd stretched the truth. "Would you like to go inside?"

"You can't just walk into someone's house."

"In this case, I can."

Her curiosity shifted to confusion. "I'm not going in without asking."

"I already asked. It's not a problem."

Ty took her hand and led her to the front door. He pulled out the door key and turned the lock. Mandy's eyes widened while she shook her head. "I'm not comfortable with this, Ty."

"It's perfectly fine Mandy. Trust me."

Though she still hesitated, he clasped her hand and encouraged her to step inside. When she barely budged, he feared he would have to drag her in. The idea made him tighten his jaw to stop himself from laughing.

She finally stepped inside, and her main focus was the Christmas tree. "Ty, the tree is gorgeous."

She moved closer and gazed at the ornaments one by one. "I love the ornaments."

"It is pretty. So, what do you think of the house?"

"First, it's huge. No one needs a house this big."

"That depends. If they have lots of friends or family maybe they do need the room."

"I suppose." But she didn't sound convinced.

Ty beckoned her. "Come closer, I want to show you something." His voice sounded weak but he understood why. In a moment, he would do something that would change his life. "Look at that limb." He pointed, and she eyed a gold key ring with a red bow.

She gazed at it, but turned away. Though he could see he'd aroused her interest, she stayed back as if not understanding.

"Hand it to me, Mandy. I want to show you something."

"Me? No. It's your neighbor's. I'm not touching it."

He managed to stop a laugh but realized his request was hopeless. "This is for you, Mandy."

Her head snapped back. "What? How can it be for me when it's on your neighbor's tree?"

"No, it's on my tree, Mandy."

Her jaw dropped, and she gaped at him and then the key ring. "What? How can this be your house, and you've never mentioned it?" She spun around her eyes shifting one way and then the other. "You're not making any sense."

He sensed she didn't comprehend his little joke, his plan failed. Mandy didn't find humor in what he'd done. He'd been distorting the truth in too many ways. "Mandy, I've been playing games with you, and I'm sorry. This is too important to confuse you. I'm not going crazy. Let me explain."

"I wish you would, Ty. I'm so confused that nothing is making sense."

"This is really my house. I didn't tell you about it, because I wanted to surprise you, although I didn't want to confuse you so much that learning the truth makes you angry, and I fear that's what I've done."

"You're right, Ty. I'm not angry exactly, but I don't understand why you didn't tell me you owned a house, a gorgeous house like this one. Why keep it a secret?"

"One of the reasons is that you'd put so much work into your grandmother's house, and I felt as if showing you this one might come across as showing off. Obviously, this house is larger, but in my opinion, both houses are attractive and useful. Both will meet the needs of a family, and Mandy, one other reason I didn't mention the house—I believed I couldn't tell you without ruining something even more important."

"What could be more important, Ty?"

"Remember how you always say I had a surprise up my sleeve. Well, this time it's really up my sleeve."

"And that's important? Something this important doesn't make sense, Ty."

"I made a mistake, a big one, but maybe you'll understand if what I do now makes sense."

He studied her expression, praying she would understand. "Mandy, we both know that our friendship has grown dramatically. I hope you agree with me, because I've felt it for a long time." He grasped her hand and searched her amazing eyes as rounded as a full moon.

"I agree, Ty, and that's why I was hurt when I learned about the house and realized you kept it a secret. Two people as close as we've become can't keep secrets. Keeping a special gift a secret makes sense, but..." She lay her palm on his jaw and cupped his chin in her hand. "We've talked about the importance of communication, and that secret hurt me. Maybe I'm overly sensitive, but my parents had poor communication, and..." She choked on the words. "I know, we aren't like my parents, I know but—"

"But it's important, Mandy. I can understand now, so forgive me. I promise you that I'll be sensitive about no secrets, and I hope you trust me. So much has happened in your life these past few months, and we want to be open and honest. I'll never lie to you. I never have and never will."

She lowered her head and moved closer to him. When she raised her eyes, she gave him a faint smile. "Thank you, Ty." She studied the key ring a moment. "Since it is your Christmas tree, I'll do as you asked." She lifted the key ring from the limb and studied it. "It opens something." Her forehead wrinkled as she turned it over in her hand. "Should I guess?"

He slipped his arm around her waist. "Give it a try."

Mandy grinned. "It's the key to your heart. Am I right?"

"Mandy my love, it's that too, but it's also the key to our house."

"Our house? If it really were I would love it, Ty."

He reached up his sleeve and pulled out a tiny box. "Now, this surprise is legitimate since it was really up my sleeve. He moved closer, slipped the ring from the velvet box and knelt at her feet. "Mandy, would you be not only my best friend but also my wife?"

She stared at the lovely gold and diamond engagement ring and raised her eyes to Ty. "I've waited for you to ask for years. I love you with all my heart, and I want to be your best friend and your loving wife. You've made me happy for years, and I long to share the rest of our lives together."

"Forever, my love. Forever." He rose and slipped the ring on her finger. She looked into his eyes and kissed him the way she'd always longed to do. "I love you with my heart and soul, Ty."

"I love you, Mandy, more than I can express. I want you to be my wife, and I don't want to wait. We've waited too long."

"We have, Ty, and knowing where our lives are headed. This is my best Christmas ever."

"And mine too. I told my parents my plan to ask you to be my wife, and they were thrilled, Mandy. Though you haven't had the joy of two parents who loved each other, you now have two who love each other and you."

Tears misted Mandy's eyes. "Thank you for sharing them, and I'm thrilled they're happy for us."

"Mandy, I want to explain one more thing. When we were talking about the houses, yours and this one, remember I said that both houses will meet the needs of a family. What I said meant more than it sounded. I want us to be a family, Mandy. You'll be a wonderful mother and I want to be a good father."

"You'll be an amazing father, Ty. You have a great role model."

"Thank you, my love. I am blessed with a fine dad and mom, but what I want you to know is I really mean that either house will meet our needs. I'll live in either house that you prefer. I know your grandmother's house means a lot to you. This one brings with it no memories or connection to family. Please decide and that's where we'll live."

"I can't make that decision now, even if I wanted to. My mind and heart are full. You've asked me to marry you, and I had the answer. Yes. Yes, with all my heart. I hope we can wait a while until we both decide where we will live, and which home will be best for our family. So, no more questions. Please.

Ty's chest tightened. He'd been holding back questions that he longed to ask, but didn't want to ruin the beautiful moment. "I'd like to ask you a few things, but they can wait. You're right. Let's enjoy these moments that we'll always remember. Questions can be answered another day."

Mandy sensed his questions were important. They needed to be open and honest with each other just as they'd discussed, and his concerns must have been important for him to mention them. "Ty, please ask me the questions. Marriage means not only loving, but sharing and communicating. Don't hold back.

He searched her face and could almost read her thoughts, her attitude on love and marriage. "I wondered if…" He lowered his head as if looking away could erase his concern.

"Ty, ask me, please."

His pulse skipped, but instead of waiting, he dragged out his question and asked. "Will you tell your mother about our engagement? I know things haven't always been good with the two of you, but—"

"Thanks for caring, Ty. Yes, I want to forgive my mother. I'm sorry that I didn't understand what happened in her life and what happened between my mother and dad. But I know now, and it's time to forgive."

"I'm more than pleased, Mandy. I know it's too late for your dad to be part of your change of heart, but I hope in heaven he knows what's happened."

Her eyes misted again, but this time, she loved what he'd said. His love of family meant the world to her. "Thank you, Ty, for caring and loving. You are an amazing man."

"And you're even more amazing, my soon-to-be wife."

♥

Mandy sat beside Ty in front of the fireplace in his lovely house, the house she would choose as their home. She studied the short list, a list that made her happy. She and Ty had agreed they didn't want to wait. They'd already waited a lifetime.

She handed Ty the notepad and hoped that he would remember old friends, especially her grandmother's who she wanted to invite. "Who else, Ty?"

He ran his finger down the paper and shrugged. "I think you have everyone. You wanted a small wedding, and this is it as far as I can see." He scanned the sheet again. She'd listed his parents first, then her grandmother's old friend, Edith and she'd even slipped in Lauren. "He'd review one more time and saw her mother's name near the end. Seeing her listed, touched him. She'd really forgiven her mother. "And what about those cousins? Dena and—"

"And Gwen." She gave him a wink. "I should. Then they could see our home."

Ty's brows curved like the Gateway Arch in St. Louis. "I hope you're kidding."

Mandy didn't respond except for a silly grin which told him she was joking. "Ty, help me remember those two neighbors of grandma's who helped so much at the funeral luncheon. Edith's on the list already. I'm thinking of..." She snapped her fingers. "Was it Betsy?"

"Right, I remember that name."

"I'm pretty sure that's one of the names, but then there was..."

"Hazel. I remember that name because Hazel is one

of my mom's aunts."

"Thanks. What about your store manager?"

"Whew. How could I forget Matt?

She jotted down the new names. "He has a wife, doesn't he?"

"Teresa. I'm glad you thought of them. He would be upset to be forgotten."

"So would the Johnsons. They were grandma's long-time neighbors, too."

Ty stared at the list again. "What about Al Green? You just saw him recently, and I know you were good friends in high school."

"That's getting a bit raucous, but you're right. Let's cut it off here. The only people I still question is Dena and Gwen. I'm having second thoughts."

"If you insist, Mandy, but that's it, okay?"

She shrugged and re-checked the list. "Unless we think of someone important that's it. Promise."

"And you're sure about the date, Mandy? It might be hard to have it on Christmas Eve. Lots of people visit relatives or have family dinners. I like the idea, but as I think about it, we might get married with my parent's and no one else."

She thought a moment before responding. "We're having an afternoon wedding with a lunch instead of dinner. Let's hope it works."

Ty tossed the decision around in his head and gave up. He'd suggested New Year's Eve, and Mandy rejected that, so he agreed about Christmas Eve day and let it go. The wedding meant more to them than the guests, and it was in the Lord's hands as far as Ty was concerned.

As the day's ticked past, Mandy sent out invitations,

and had to break her promise. Al had called her about one of her high school friends who wanted to see her. When she met Abby for lunch, she asked her to be her bride's maid. She'd forgotten about that tradition and Al had been dating Abby so it made sense. Mandy planed the catered lunch and added a few more Christmas decorations to the living room and dining room. The fireplace mantel held her grandmother's collection of angels. Seeing them in the attic, Mandy took them to the new house grateful she'd found them. They were a major remembrance of Christmas at her grandmother's.

The snowfall became deep as the wind blew the snow into piles. Ty tried to keep them off the sidewalks and driveway, but the battle wasn't easy, and he wished he'd strung the lights around the doorway and the bushes on each side of the door before the snow had fallen.

Each day the postmen delivered the wedding RSVPs and all of them so far indicated their attendance. At the last minute, she'd sent an invitation to Dena and Gwen while she prayed they wouldn't cause a ruckus and ruin her wedding.

Ty's mother had accompanied Mandy when she shopped for a wedding dress. Mandy wanted something attractive, but not the typical flouncy dress with a train and veil a young bride would wear. She'd had her thirty-second birthday in February. In a few weeks, she would be another year older.

Though Ty had worried about their wedding guests being unable to attend, he'd been wrong. Every day his heart fluttered, anxious and excited that he and Mandy would soon be Mr. and Mrs. Evans, a dream he'd had for years, and Mandy admitted the same. They proved that best friends can fall in love.

On Christmas Eve day, a bustle of activities resounded in the house. The caterers had arrived, His parents rang the doorbell two hours before the wedding, and Mandy's mother showed up with a smile. She pitched in, to his surprise, and the signs of forgiveness filled the air. Ty was grateful, and Mandy's expression let him know that she'd made a wise decision.

The minister came to the door, sharing his story of getting stuck in a snowdrift and a kind young man helped him get out safely.

The large living room provided a cozy yet ample space for the wedding. The fireplace looked perfect with the angels and four lit candles adding more Christmas spirit. At three o'clock, the guests were seated, the minister stood in front of the fireplace, the Christmas tree towered in the corner covered in white lights and an angel tree topper. The room looked beautiful.

Ty and Matt, his store manager, serving as his best man, stood on the right side of the fireplace, as a recording played, *It Came Upon A Midnight Clear*. Mandy waited until Abby appeared in the archway and moved to the left side of the fireplace.

The music changed to *Silent Night*, and Mandy, wearing an ivy-colored dress and carrying a bouquet of red roses draped with holly and ivy glided down the aisle and stood beside Abby. The wedding service began with prayers and a short sermon based on 1 Corinthians.

Love is patient, love is kind. It does not envy, it does not boast, it is not proud. It does not dishonor, it is not self-seeking, it is not easily angered, it keeps no record of wrongs. Love does not delight in evil but rejoices with the truth. It always protects, always trusts, always hopes, always perseveres. Love never fails. And now these three remain: faith, hope and love. But the greatest of these is love.

The wedding vows began, and when the pastor spoke the words, "You are now husband and wife. You may kiss the bride," Mandy held her breath eager to hear the final words. "I give you, Mr. and Mrs. Tyler Evans."

Everyone applauded, and they were surrounded by family and friends. Her mother held back, but following Ty's parents, she congratulated them and hugged Mandy. To Mandy's surprise, her mother even hugged Ty.

When the caterers announced the meal, everyone moved into the dining room where the food was spread out on the buffet. Baked chicken, tossed salad, a potato casserole, fresh-baked dinner rolls and a corn dish vanished as the wedding guests enjoyed the menu. The three-tiered wedding cake was covered with white butter cream icing and decorated with red roses, holly berries and ivy.

As hours ticked by, the guests began to leave, and when her mother indicated she was leaving, Mandy asked her to stay a bit longer so they could talk. She agreed although she seemed eager to go.

Before Mandy had the opportunity to speak privately with her mother, Dena and Gwen cornered her with the same insults and demands she had listened to before. Her patience vanished, and her attempt to be kind faded. "Ladies, I'd like to remind you that this is my wedding day. Would you please keep your warped view of who you are and who I am, and let it go?"

Dena bustled toward her, her face only an inch away. "Just because you're rich, and don't say you aren't, you can't tell us what we think."

She shook her head, frustrated that they were doing their best to ruin her wedding day.

"Gwen and Dena, if you recall, you are not related to my grandmother. You are not an heir and I can't rewrite the will. But I will tell you something so you might learn." Mandy drew in a breath fighting for air. "Ladies I am giving my mother my grandmother's house since Ty owns this beautiful one that you're in at this moment. I had planned to sell the house and share the money with my mother and a portion of it to you, but I've changed my mind."

Dena jammed her face into Mandy's again. "You're doing what? What right do you have to tell me—"

"Every right in this world, Dena. Every right. You have no rights, and with your attitude, I'm glad I hadn't said I would share anything with you. I've tried to be kind to most everyone, ladies, but it's difficult to be kind to you. My mother and I had some issues, but we understood the concept of forgiveness and kindness and love. Those are a blessing."

"We've thought about suing you, Amanda, but I've stopped thinking about it, because, I'm doing it. You just wait."

"Dena, I hate to break the news, but suing me will cost you more money than you'd get if that were possible. But you can't win, and I can. If you're anxious to give me money, go right ahead. But be prepared. I'm not going to put up with you anymore, either of you. I'm sorry it's turned out this way, but you've given me no choice."

Mandy tried to swallow her frustration, but she couldn't. They once again ruined her day and this was a day that she hoped to remember with happiness.

She turned and pointed to the door. "So I can enjoy my wedding reception, I'm asking you to leave, and if you'd rather not, I'll have Ty escort you outside. This is enough." She made another gesture toward the door. "Goodbye, Ladies." Mandy turned her back to them and walked away. Her last image of the sisters was two mouths hanging open like hungry baby birds.

♥

Ty saw the cousins acting up again, and his frustration overtook his desire to be nice but firm. These women seemed to listen with dead ears. He shifted closer to them and followed them toward the door. When Dena appeared to inch her way toward Mandy again, Ty passed them and grabbed the doorknob. "This way ladies, and I might ask you not to come here again. If you do, we'll have to handle this in an unkind way and Mandy and I aren't unkind people."

Dena gaped at him but didn't move. He'd had enough of the two of them to give up. "One more time, Dena. Goodbye." Dena didn't budge, but Gwen did and he had an idea. "Gwen, you seem to be the one with intelligence and common sense. Today is our wedding day, and I don't think you want to be the guests who will be remembered by everyone for trying to ruin this precious day."

Gwen winced at his words, and for the first time since they arrived, he had hoped. Gwen faced Dena and tilted her head toward the door. "Give them a break, Dena. I think they've put up with enough. If I were in their shoes, I would have called the police."

"Police." Dena's voice echoed through the room while people faced her, their jaws hanging.

Gwen spun around, grabbed her coat and marched outside. Before Dena could follow, Gwen hurried to her car and pulled away. Dena gaped at her sister as she vanished down the street. Her head swiveled from person to person, until she faced Ty.

"How am I going to get home?"

Everyone turned away and ignored her tantrum, except Ty. "Call a taxi, Dena, and tell them to hurry. I'm tired of listening to your ridiculous rage, and I want you gone. I'm sorry I agreed to invite you to our wedding. Mandy has a good heart and wanted to show kindness, but some people don't know how to accept it."

"But you really don't want me to take a taxi. You could drive me hom—"

"Goodbye, Dena."

She gaped at him, shock darkening her face, but he ignored her and walked away. The woman had no idea that the world didn't revolve around her threats and her poor-little-me attitude. His heart lifted when he saw a taxi pull up to the house.

When he looked for Mandy, he spotted her with her mother standing in what he called the sunroom. Today the sun glinted off the snow piles and yet a warmth covered the wintery day. He had a wife, a beautiful, kind woman whom he'd loved forever and today they had vowed their true love, a love that needed no vow. Throughout their years as best friends, they'd proved their forever love.

When he looked up, Mandy beckoned to him, but he didn't move not wanting to interfere with her time with her mother. When she insisted, and her mother smiled, he did as Mandy asked.

"Thank you, Mrs. Cahill. I'm so glad that—"

"Ty, please call me Trina. I won't ask you to call me mother." She gave him a wink.

He glanced at Mandy, and she slipped her arm around his waist. "Mom, and I had a good talk, Ty, but she doesn't want the house."

His head jerked back. "Why? It's a very nice house, Mandy and I painted it and replaced some—"

Trina rested her hand on his shoulder. "Ty, you have been good to me, and I don't deserve it. Mandy has forgiven me, and apparently so have you. But I haven't forgiven myself. I could have explained how I messed up my life, and in messing up mine, I did the same to Mandy's dad and Mandy too."

Ty drew closer. "But that's in the past. It would make us happy to have you use the house. It's comfortable and a nice size for one or two people."

She reached up and gave him a hug while he stood there startled at her response.

"I already told Mandy that I've been working, and I have a good salary and a savings. For the first time in my life, I'm proud of me and I'm proud of both of you."

Ty didn't understand so he didn't know what to say. "Thank you." Those were the only words he could think of. Mandy eyed him. "Ty, Mom is right. She's proud of her life now and I don't want to change that. All she wants now is what we've given her already. Forgiveness."

Tears moistened in Trina's eyes, and Ty understood, and he knew Mandy did too. Mandy slipped her arms around her mother's waist. "Today is extra special. Not only do I have an amazing husband, but I have a mother who wants to visit and be a grandmother to our children."

Ty gave a nod. "I'm really happy, Trina, and I'm anxious to be a daddy. Mandy and I have agreed that we've waited a long time to get married. Too long. We're not going to make that mistake again. My goal is to have a little one by next Christmas. It'll be the best Christmas ever."

Mandy looked at her mother, knowing her mother was ready too. "Will you babysit, Mom?

"You know I will, and I'd be terribly hurt if you didn't ask me." She turned to Ty and gave him a hug. "I know I have competition but it's settled. Mr. and Mrs. Evans agreed to take turns."

Mandy couldn't stop her chuckle. "I hope this excitement doesn't change. Ty, you and I are blessed. Built in babysitters fighting for their turn."

They all laughed, and when they'd stopped laughing, Mandy turned her head toward the Christmas tree, her heart full. "You know what Ty, next year will be the best Christmas we'll ever have." She leaned in and gave him a kiss that she would never forget.

Merry Christmas to you all

Dear Reader,

You are important to us. Without you our books would not have an audience so thank you. If you enjoyed **any of my recent books**, such as Love in the Air or Sedona Sunset, one thing you could do to help promote this novel or any you enjoy, please write a short review or few comments on Amazon. Thanks so much.

You are invited to subscribe to my newsletter which comes out bi-monthly with photos, news, appearances, a recipe, book info and a devotional. Visit http://www.gailgaymermartin.com and find the subscription in the right sidebar on the home page.

I love to hear from readers and thank you for enjoying books.

Gail Gaymer Martin

About Gail
Best-selling and award-winning novelist, Gail Gaymer Martin is the author of contemporary romance and romantic suspense with 83 published novels and over four million books sold. Her novels have won numerous national awards, including: the ACFW Carol Award, RT Reviewer's Choice Award and Booksellers Best. Gail is the author of Writer Digest's *Writing the Christian Romance.* She is a founder of American Christian Fiction Writers and a member of Advanced

Speakers and Writers. Gail is a keynote speaker at churches, civic and business organizations and a workshop presenter at conferences across the U.S. She lives with husband Bob in Sedona, AZ. Contact her by mail at: PO Box 20054, Sedona, AZ 86341 or on her website or social media.

Website:www.gailgaymermartin.com
Facebook:www.facebook.com/gail.g.martin.3
Twitter:http://twitter.com/GailGMartin
GoodReads: http://bit.ly/1e8Gt6D
LinkedIn: www.linkedin.com/in/gailgaymermartin

Gail's Books from Winged Publication

Novels - *Reissues*
Dreaming of Castles 2014
Out On A Limb 2016
Over Her Head 2017
Love Comes To Butterfly Tree Inn 2017
A Love Unforeseen 2017
Loving Treasures
Loving Hearts
Loving Ways
Loving Care
Loving Promises
Loving Kisses
Loving Arms
Teacher's Pet (Former: Dad in Training)

Novels - New
Treasures Of Her Heart 2014
Romance By Design 2015
Mackinac Island Christmas 2017
Love in the Air

Novellas   Reissues
An Open Door
Apples Of His Eye
Better To See You
Once A Stranger
Then Came Darkness
To Keep Me Warm
True Riches
Yuletide Treasures

Novellas - New
Lattes and Love Songs 2015
Apple Blossom Daze 2016
A Trip To Remember 2016
A Tucumcari Christmas 2016
Poppy Fields and You, 2017
Love Comes to Butterfly Tree Inn 2017
Tumbling Into Love 2017
Lost In Red Rock Country 2017
Autumn's Fresh Beginnings 2017

Collections
Christmas Potpourri
Forget Me Not Romances #1
Forget Me Not Romances #2
Love Blooms In The Here & Now
Mocha Marriage
Romance Across the Globe
Romance On The Run
Seven Mysterious Ladies
With This Ring
A Kiss is Still a Kiss
Get Your Kiss On Route 66
Valentine Matchmakers
All Mixed Up
Love In Danger

California
Second Change At Love
When Love Calls
The Hope of Christmas
Happily Ever After
Romancing The Wild
Returning Home
Coming Home Again
Songs of the Heart
Fall N' For You
Stranded

Made in the USA
Monee, IL
07 December 2024

72753217R00104